Shiv Kumar Sharma

THE MAN & HIS MUSIC

Shiv Kumar Sharma
THE MAN & HIS MUSIC

Edited by
Ina Puri

NIYOGI
BOOKS

Published by
NIYOGI BOOKS
D-78, Okhla Industrial Area, Phase-I
New Delhi-110 020, India
Tel: 91-11-26816301, 49327000
Fax: 91-11-26810483, 26813830
email: niyogibooks@gmail.com
www.niyogibooksindia.com

Design: Write Media

ISBN: 978-93-83098-14-9
Year of Publication: 2014

Printed at: Niyogi Offset Pvt. Ltd., New Delhi, India

Contents

Foreword

Music has played a central role in my life from my childhood. Having first heard Dogri songs and bhajans from my mother, who came from a small village in Himachal Pradesh, then going on to learning classical music from the age of ten at my father's behest. He was a connoisseur of Indian classical music and arranged for me to start learning regularly from an early age. My tutor was Balram Singh Rawat and, on two summers, Ustad Vilayat Hussain Khan of the Agra Gharana came to instruct me.

After a break of several years, I found myself as the head of state in Jammu and Kashmir in three different capacities – first as Regent, then as Sadre-i-Riyasat and then as Governor. It was at this stage that I decided to restart my music lessons. It so happened that the main pujari of our family temples in Jammu, Pandit Uma Dutt Sharma, was a remarkable storehouse of classical music. He started coming to my residence thrice a week, and with him often came his young son, Shiv Kumar.

Even as a boy, Shiv initially showed extraordinary talent in playing the tabla at which he achieved great skill. In fact, the first time that I arranged for him to attend the Sur Sangeet Sansad in Bombay, it was for the tabla. Meanwhile, his father had placed in his hands an instrument that had so far been used only in Kashmiri sufiyana music, known as the santoor. The rest, as they say, is history. Shiv Kumar improved the instrument by adding various elements so that it could be used in Hindustani classical music, and subsequently became famous around the world for his extraordinary skill in the santoor. Shiv Kumar Sharma, therefore, has made a unique contribution to Hindustani music by introducing a new instrument and presenting it with utmost skill and dedication.

L to R: Yasho Rajya Lakshmi, Dr Karan Singh, Ina Puri, Pandit Shiv Kumar Sharma and Anindo Chatterjee.

As a boy, Shiv was very handsome, and it has been a pleasure to see him grow into a really impressive maestro. The credit for this goes essentially to his father, Pandit Uma Dutt Sharma, who trained him from childhood. It is interesting to note that Jammu produced another father and son duo – Ustad Allah Rakha and his son Zakir Hussain, who is probably the best percussionist in India today. I have often had occasion listening to Pandit Shiv Kumar accompanied by Zakir Hussain, a combination that is truly unforgettable and reflects the divinity inherent in music.

I am glad that this book on 'Shiv Kumar Sharma: The Man & His Music' carrying a number of family and historic photographs is being brought out to introduce him to a wider audience in India and abroad. I am sure this will be greatly appreciated by his many admirers. I take this opportunity to wish him many more years of great music performances. His son, Rahul, is also now beginning to follow in his father's footsteps.

Dr Karan Singh
New Delhi, 06.09.2013

'This kind of musician probably comes along once in a few hundred years,' observes Ustad Zakir Hussain.

Introduction

In the aftermath of 1947, the years after India met its historic tryst with destiny, what we now refer to as the post-colonial years, the country witnessed a virtual renaissance of the arts. Across the country, at homely *baithak*s (interactive sessions) or at music *sammelan*s (grand gatherings), a generation of musicians enthralled discerning listeners with their spectacular performances, winning accolades and admiration time and again. In those glorious eras, different *gharana*s (family or house, typically refers to the place where the musical ideology originated) established their distinctive styles, each unique in its own way. Distinguished maestros such as Baba Allauddin Khan had legendary disciples in Ustad Ali Akbar Khan, Pandit Ravi Shankar, Annapurna Devi, among others. Elsewhere, there was Ustad Hafiz Ali Khan, Ustad Bismillah Khan, Ustad Vilayat Khan, who mesmerised the attentive listeners (that often included other musicians), their formidable oeuvre taking Indian classical music to hitherto unsurpassed levels of excellence. While the history of classical music was being written by these illustrious greats, in Jammu, a young boy was pondering why his father and guru, Pandit Uma Dutt Sharma, had gifted him a complex instrument he had chanced upon in Srinagar. After all, from his earliest recollection, he was trained to be a tabla player and had on many occasions accompanied the most renowned instrumentalists and vocalists on the tabla for All India Radio, Jammu & Kashmir, where his father was in charge of the classical music section.

This book seeks to capture the extraordinary life and times of Padma Vibhushan Pandit Shiv Kumar Sharma and his journey with the santoor. How will the history of Indian classical music regard the contribution of Pandit Shiv Kumar Sharma? His has been a career spanning six decades

Pandit Shiv Kumar Sharma at a fund-raiser in London, with (L to R) Rahul Sharma, Satish Vyas, Ina Puri, Manjit Bawa and Ustad Shafaat Ahmed Khan.

where he has achieved the distinction of single-handedly establishing the santoor on the world map as an instrument of Indian classical music. In the process, he has given it the identity it lacked in its past, where the santoor was used primarily as an accompaniment in a folk ensemble. The journey of the struggle that shows the steely resolve and determination to succeed come what may is framed against the background of the newly independent country that is in the throes of Nehruvian optimism. Everywhere, there is hope. Hope in Shivji's case is a precarious mental conditioning that is unwilling to submit to failures and defeat no matter how trying the circumstances. Therefore, with little money but high on the hope quotient, when the young man makes his way to Bombay (now Mumbai) with no idea how he is to begin his career, he is overjoyed to see a crumbling edifice with the sign Kashmir Hotel! He considers it a good omen and disembarks from his horse carriage, takes up his modest lodgings and steps out to see what life has in store for him.

Circa 2013, as Pandit Shiv Kumar Sharma crosses another threshold, his seventy-fifth birthday, it is time to revisit his life and musical journey. Observing him from the very beginning of his career, Pandit Vijay Kichlu, himself a well-renowned practitioner, has had the privilege of being a close friend of Shivji's down the decades. He talks about Shivji's music as only an insider could, throwing light upon the complexities of the instrument and how Shivji was able to finally achieve the phenomenal success he has. In another section, we have Manek Premchand sharing his in-depth knowledge as a film historian on

Before Rahul's first concert in Kolkata in 1999.

Shivji's long and fascinating contribution to Hindi film music, as a musician as well as a music director, using the pseudonym Shiv Hari.

My own interview is a dialogue that weaves in and out of diverse subjects. As his biographer, it has been an honour to be associated with Shivji for over two decades, working on his memoirs and the documentary that fetched us the Rajat Kamal. It was fitting that the past books and film should be followed by a volume that not only focussed on his life textually but also through rare archival photographs from the family's personal collection.

The Foreword has been written by the distinguished scholar Dr Karan Singh, who happens to be Shivji's guru bhai as a disciple of his father in Jammu. The Epilogue is by his son and disciple Rahul Sharma, a musician of repute, who will carry on the legacy he has inherited to even greater heights. I am deeply grateful to Dayanita Singh who very kindly gave us permission to use the photographs she has taken of Shivji's in the long time that she has known him. I would like to thank Avinash Pasricha for his photographs. I would also like to express my gratitude to Ravi Mathur and ITC Sangeet Research Academy for sharing rare, archivally invaluable photographs from their collection. Last but not the least, my deep gratitude to Tultul and Bikash Niyogi for commissioning this book and their generous support.

Ina Puri
Gurgaon, 2013

Pandit Shiv Kumar Sharma and Ina Puri at Rajeev Apartments, Mumbai.

In Conversation with Ina Puri

With sons Rohit and Rahul, and biographer Ina Puri at the release of Journey with a Hundred Strings: My Life in Music *in Mumbai.*

IP: This is a continuation of the dialogue we had initiated some twenty years ago, the same dialogue that resulted in our shared memoir, *Journey with a Hundred Strings: My Life in Music*—a book that not only ran into several editions, but was thereafter translated into Marathi and Hindi. In the following years, our creative collaboration resulted in *Antardhwani*, a documentary directed by Jabbar Patel, which won the National Award. This conversation, in a sense, picks up the thread to earlier dialogues spanning the last two decades. During this period, I have seen you quietly and gradually withdraw into a space wherein to meditate and retrospect, delving into the soul and creating music that has reached newer heights.

SKS: You have indeed been a witness to my life and the journey. As far as distancing myself is concerned, that too is true. Distancing is a process of connecting with the *antardhwani*, the voice within.

IP: You are distancing yourself from the chaos and the confusion that we see around us, where the music industry is concerned, where life is concerned, where different distractions are concerned. None of it bothers you. You are in a world where you're creating music; you're spending time with Rahul; you're praying to your God. You are in a space which is almost like you're in the Himalayas.

'Earlier there was a struggle to be accepted ... Today, a music conference is incomplete without the participation of Shivji.'
Pandit Bhimsen Joshi

SKS: I have been like this from the very beginning. Indian classical music is spiritually inclined, for its base is spiritualism. So right from the time when I was learning music, I was given these spiritual values by my father who was also my guru. The western concept of music is different. There, they only look at music, whether it is pop or classical or whatever genre, as entertainment. The entire philosophy of Indian classical music, on the other hand, has evolved based on spirituality because in our ancient culture, sound was not seen just as a musical note, but as vibrations in the universe as well as in the elements. Later, music became professional and the focus changed. It was now performed in front of people to get their appreciation. You had to please the listeners who happened to be rajas, maharajas, nawabs. The whole perspective changed. In this changed world, when we talk about Indian classical music, it is supposed to be viewed as a spiritual pursuit ... But what is spirituality?

IP: When you're talking about the spiritual aspect vis-à-vis Indian classical music, how can you make this comment? You are aware how Indian classical music today is veering on the same path, seeking to please, to excite and to entertain.

SKS: For me, when I'm sitting in my room and doing my riyaz (practice), this music gives me a certain kind of bliss. And I experience the same bliss when I'm playing on stage, whether there are two hundred or twenty thousand people listening.

IP: So who do you play for?

SKS: I share that bliss with my audience. They can only share it when they connect with me. It is like sitting in meditation. What connects with me is not the knowledge of a classical raga or *taal* (tempo). These are technicalities. Recently I've been doing this experiment with students, particularly in colleges. When I play the *alap* (cadence), I tell them, 'Forget about me, Shiv Kumar Sharma, forget about the santoor, forget about the raga. Just close your eyes.' The moment you close your eyes, you start getting different ideas that are not connected with one another. The only effort you have to make is to bring back your thoughts towards that sound. I don't call it a raga, santoor, *taal* or anything else. And I find extraordinary reactions from people. I'm surprised. So this is my way of thinking and presenting my music.

IP: But you don't really present your music. You're merely sharing your music.

SKS: That's what I'm saying. I'm sharing it with my audience. What I'm sharing is the bliss that music is giving to me. However, they will have to walk that extra mile to experience it.

IP: When you say presentation, I have a problem with the word because you don't present your music. You don't even have a sequence in your mind. I have seen and I have heard from you that when you're sitting on the stage, the creativity, the process of creation, happens on the spot. And you have often referred to yourself as a medium. So in that sense, there is no presentation.

SKS: Exactly.

IP: It's a spontaneous flow.

SKS: Spirituality is not only in the context of music, it is in your life, in your behaviour, in your activities, you live it. There are three words: *man* (thought), *vachan* (speech), *karam* (action). I'll elaborate on this. Now, this is besides music, because your music is what you are. Your personality is what your thinking is and your philosophy is what your emotions are. All these things come out in your music. This is what I'm trying to practice. It's very hard, but I have been trying to practice it for many years. What I think, whatever my philosophy or my thoughts are, I should have the courage to speak that out. You know, sometimes we are thinking something else and not saying it because we are being politically correct. Our philosophy is something else, but we are presenting something else. So then *man* and *vachan* are not on the same wavelength.

Spirituality means that your thoughts, speech and actions match. I'm experiencing it more and more and trying to follow

IRA LANDGARTEN

it. So when your thinking is like that, the perspective of your music is bound to change; your behaviour will also change. Suppose I deliver an interesting lecture about philosophy of a certain kind, but I don't follow it personally, then I'm just a professional speaker. I inspire people; I have got that gift to impress people with my talk and inspire them. But I am myself not doing that. Once I finish that speech, I come home and do something else. *Man, vachan, karam* have not connected. It is the same in music.

Honesty in your actions ultimately reaches the people who get connected with you or who experience your music or your thoughts. This is what I tell my students as well, but it's not easy. I'll give an example. There could be a musician who is more popular than I am, XYZ, anybody. And in my heart of hearts, I know that. But I don't have the courage to accept it publicly. So the equilibrium between thought, speech and action is lacking.

IP: In a recent incident in Pune, your concert with Zakir Hussain was advertised as a *jugalbandi* (a duet of two solo musicians). I recall the fact that even though your attention was drawn to it, you were fine ... this despite the incorrect connotation because Zakir Hussain was such a star in his own right and you understood that the organisers were trying to cash in on his image and appearance, not as an accompanist but as a co-player.

SKS: There is a lot of confusion here; we have to learn to draw the line. Some people get mixed up; they think ego is confidence, which it is not. Confidence comes from surrender. That gives you power. Ego, on the other hand, is something that relates to 'I'. So what we have to do as musicians is to accept that I'm only a medium, and I have a responsibility. Medium doesn't mean that you are a machine and somebody will switch it on and it will start. You have to make an effort. To realise that you are no more than a medium needs a lot of *sadhana* (practice), meditation and thinking. You have to practice what you think.

It's very hard, but once you understand that and you surrender, then some divine power takes over. This has happened with me throughout my career.

Sometimes people ask me that you didn't have a reference point about the santoor when you started playing this instrument, how did you create this style? I share with them what happened during my career at different points in time. I learned from my father, I started playing with him and he gave me the basic technique, he taught me the raga, *taal* and so on. But, for the rest of the things, I really didn't have any reference point. Nobody had played the santoor in the classical style, only the Sufi musicians were playing the santoor and I wasn't playing that kind of music. Each instrument has got what we call in musical terms a *baaj*, a different style of playing. My style evolved during my practice sessions or while playing in front of an audience. When I played something instantaneously, I would realise that I had not practiced this. After the concert or session, I said to myself, okay, this is also possible. Then I started working on that. It has now been sixty years—I started as a santoor player on the radio in 1952—but I feel right from the start that some divine force was giving me ideas. And I also believe that ideas are stored in your mind. I have been exposed to different kinds of music, folk music from Jammu and Punjab, for instance. Hence I have not only focussed on classical music.

IP: Tell us your memories of adolescence, of growing up by the Tawi River. How did you get this exposure to folk music?

SKS: When I was a child we used to live across the river and often, at dusk, the strains of songs sung by Dogri shepherds and villagers would waft across to us. My mother used to sing folk songs as she went about her household chores and the lilting tunes of these songs stirred a strange yearning in my heart, the romance of the distant village people gripped my imagination. I used to listen to symphonies being broadcast on Radio Delhi regularly when I was in school and college. I was interested in different kinds

At a concert with the tabla maestro, Ustad Zakir Hussain.

of music, not just classical. Alongside, I was very happy playing the tabla and practicing as a vocalist till fate sent my father to Srinagar and he chanced upon the santoor and that changed my destiny.

IP: The day he told you to put aside the tabla and start playing the santoor.

His father and guru, Pandit Uma Dutt Sharma, who was an acclaimed musician and vocalist of the Banaras gharana.

SKS: Yes, and as I showed my reluctance, he told me, 'You have no idea what is going to happen with your name and the santoor. They are going to become synonymous. So you have to play this.' A few years later, Khwaja Ahmad Abbas offered me a role of one of the heroes in his film, *Saat Hindustani*. A young man could have easily been swayed but I stuck on, believing that my destiny lay in the santoor.

IP: In 1955, V Shantaram offered you a film as a music director. You were seventeen years old and you turned it down, saying your

His mother, Kesar Devi.

calling lay elsewhere. Yet, later, there came a time when apart from your classical music, you were also taking assignments to play in films. Did this cause a rift between your guru and you? After all, you had left home to carve a career in classical music. Did this flirtation with glamour anger your father?

SKS: Well, honestly, he didn't know much about what I was doing because I was broadcasting from radio as well. But he knew that I was playing for films. In all fairness, I have to admit that he was not that kind of stubborn musician who looks down upon the film industry, even though he had been asked to

Shivji was an obedient child and deeply religious. Even as a little boy he could recite the Gayatri Mantra by heart. He was drawn to music right from the start and was a devoted *shishya* [disciple] who spent hours with our father, learning the rudiments of Indian classical music, never tiring or shirking *riyaz*.

Sarla Raina

'Shivji was born much after me, after ten years in fact. There was great revelry and celebration at his birth. He was a beautiful child, very fair, with a head full of curly hair. My father, especially, adored him and kept him by his side even when he was teaching students,' recollects ***Sarla Raina*** *(Pandit Shiv Kumar Sharma's older sister).*

compose for films and act in films as well, in Lahore, which he had refused before Partition. He never told me, 'No, don't play for films.' He was confident that I was serious about my santoor and kept that faith in me.

IP: Strangely, you had no guru besides your father who guided you in the beginning and after that you were alone ... with the santoor, honing your skills and improving the tonal qualities of the instrument as you went along, with no one who could advise you.

SKS: It wasn't me, I truly believe that I was made a medium and I am blessed. As I told you, I am guided by the principles of

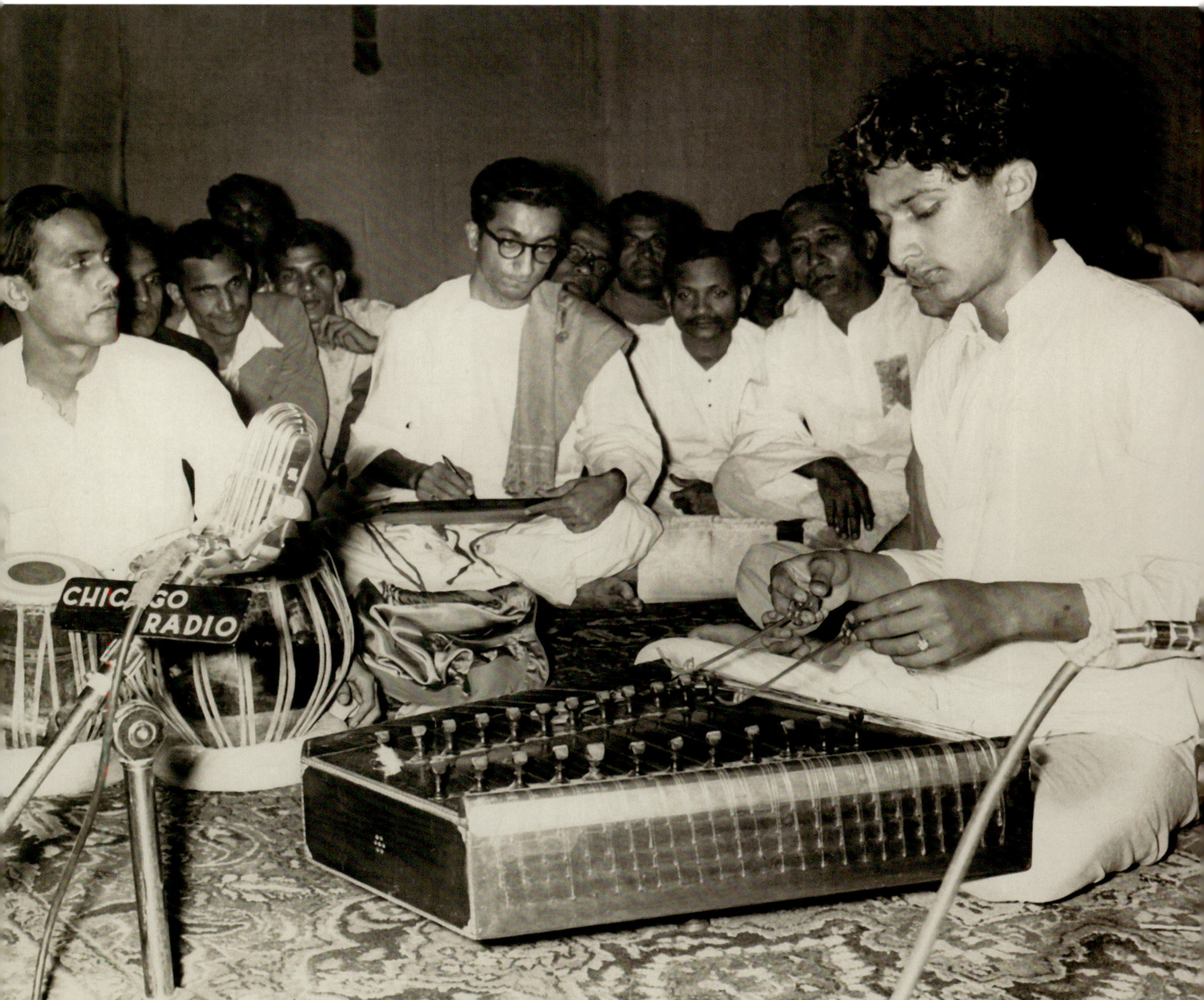

Haridas Sangeet Sammelan, Mumbai, February 1955—the first concert in Mumbai. On the tabla is Pandit Shankar Ghosh of Kolkata.

In Srinagar, around 1957, with Pandit Jasraj and Pandit Roshan Ali (seated), Assistant Station Director, Radio Srinagar.

man, vachan and *karam*. Only a person who can surrender his or her ego can accept reality. Sadly, we are tempted by materialistic achievements. If the focus shifts entirely towards materialistic achievements—fame, name, money—your creativity is bound to be compromised.

An early photograph of Pandit Shiv Kumar Sharma from the family archives.

A rare photograph capturing the young Pandit Shiv Kumar Sharma recording for Radio Kashmir.

'My parents were initially saddened at the prospect of marrying off their first-born to a musician, but my grandfather had given his word and my fate was sealed. Looking back I realise it was the best decision ...' ***Manorama Sharma***

With his parents during the wedding celebrations.

IP: But what happens about family pressures, the constant pressures from expectations? The megastars who throng the metropolis seem to relish the moment. You are, in contrast, ever restrained, at peace with yourself.

SKS: Living in the moment is a great philosophy, but we're actually not doing that. Spiritually speaking, we never live in the moment. Either we are living in the past or we are thinking about the future. We think, this is my goal, I have to reach there. We never enjoy that particular moment. You are in the present, but you are thinking about what to do, that becomes your future. This is a different philosophy, I just digressed to that. But what I mean to say is, that I never once thought of failure, of leaving the santoor and picking up the sitar or sarod; the idea just did not come to me. This is what I call divine guidance. I just never thought about it. I have never been scared of failure, despite the initial criticism and rejection, I have remained true to my goal.

'It has been a long journey together. Romance was a young girl's dream, but what kept us bonded was our respect and love for each other, no matter how trying the circumstances.'
Manorama Sharma

Lata Mangeshkar (fourth from left) after a recording session with Pandit Shiv Kumar Sharma. Padma Sachdeva seated behind Lata Mangeshkar.

IP: But divine guidance is there for every soul, every human being.

SKS: Yes, it is there, but we don't listen to it. I believe in *sanskara*, your deeds from previous lives. Maybe some people disagree with me, those who are atheists and feel there is no reincarnation, there is no previous life, there is no future. For them, there is only this life and that is why their focus is on making the best of it. But I think musicians are not made in one lifetime; musicians simply cannot be made in one lifetime. The kind of musicians who can do something different from their guru or peers are not made in one lifetime. People say, 'Oh, he's a great musician. It is in the genes.' I don't accept that theory. Genes can give you the appearance, the colour, or even diseases,

Clockwise from below: (L to R) Ustad Zakir Hussain, Abdul Halim Jaffer Khan, Manorama, Abdul Halim Jaffer Khan's daughter, Pandit Shiv Kumar Sharma and tabla player Sadashiv Pawar; On the terrace of his house in Jammu with Manorama and her friend; Performing in Jammu in early 1952.

An introspective moment by the Jhelum, Kashmir.

but not the art. It's not necessary that a great scientist's son or daughter will also be a great scientist. And why is it so? They are born in the same family; they are given the same training, the same value system, so why are they not the same? The answer is clear: because they are individual souls. This proves there is reincarnation—they bring their own karmas. Hence it is possible that a scientist's son could become a great musician. There are great musicians with two or three sons. One is extraordinary, the others are not. Why? They were given the same *taalim* (education); the same value system was imparted to them. They're different because they're different souls. So we have to understand, we are a medium, we are selected for a purpose. But just because you are selected, does not mean that everything is done. You still have to slog; you have to be honest; you have to be sincere. Sincere in thought, speech and actions—which is very, very difficult. Shiv Kumar Sharma is the name of this body, not of this soul. Tomorrow, this soul will get some other body, what we call *yantra* or machine. We have to realise that everything is transient, time is fleeting but instead of utilising our time on earth, we get distracted by petty trifles.

IP: I would like to take you back in time to the moment you stepped out of the train and found yourself in Mumbai's crowded Chattrapati Shivaji Terminus. You had taken a *tonga* and made your way to Kashmir Hotel, there was nobody you knew in the city. Circa 2013, it is a changed existence for you and the santoor. You are now recognised the world over. You have distinguished yourself, been the recipient of numerous awards/citations, yet, somewhere in the journey, do you feel that this has happened because you have chosen this path, or is it because of something you have inherited from your father or from some other life?

SKS: It's a combination of all these things. First of all, my father gave me everything—the training, the music. I must acknowledge the fact that had it not been for him, I would not have been here. Second, my dedication, my determination that kept me going through hard times when I was almost broke and on the verge of being without a place to stay in. I did not give up in spite of all this hardship. My musician friends were doing very well. They were getting concerts, I was not. I wasn't disturbed, I kept on working. And I was never affected by criticism or praise.

IP: Even then?

SKS: Yes, even then. If somebody criticised me, it was okay and if somebody praised me, that was okay, too. I had to make my own judgments. So it's a combination of all those factors as well as my philosophy that I follow. You have to be a learner all your life. You can learn something every moment from every human being, even from people who work for you and clean your house. You should always have your eyes and ears open to receive, to get something from anywhere and add it to your own thinking. I have been a learner and I am still learning as a musician, as a human being, updating myself, getting ideas and

Facing page: During a tour of America on the invitation of Pandit Ravi Shankar and George Harrison (fifth and fourth from right, seated).

Above: With Pandit Hariprasad Chaurasia and Ustad Allarakha during his America tour, 1974. Left: With Peter Sellers, Ustad Sultan Khan, Ustad Allarakha, Pandit Ravi Shankar and Pandit Hariprasad Chaurasia.

meeting people. I think the greatest learning is travelling. And there is no end to learning.

IP: Post-Independence, the euphoric Nehruvian era has given way to disenchantment. Today, people are looking for instant gratification. Even when they seek spirituality, they do so impatiently, searching for solutions at the feet of one religious

At a yoga centre in Mumbai with Dr Jaydev, his mother and wife Hansa.

guru or the other, then moving on, still thirsting for nirvana ... So what would you tell them? All around us, from Gujarat to Kashmir, there is strife. My query is, while the world simmers around you, is it possible for you to withdraw and to be able to create such moments of tranquillity for yourself? Would you not be affected by what's happening around—the war, the violence, the terrorists' attacks? Can we really detach ourselves when our world is undergoing one crisis after the other?

SKS: I'm pained by all this. As you said, the city has changed and everything is deteriorating. I think the root cause of all of these problems lies in the lack of right values. Our values have changed. When this country got freedom, the people who gave their lives and the people who took over the reins of power had different value systems. Bookish knowledge is not education; value-based knowledge is the real education. Getting a degree has become the sole purpose. Indian traditions have got great value systems but people misunderstand these and think that it is wrong to earn money or be famous. They think you should become a recluse or a sadhu and this is a wrong interpretation. You have to do everything in life—flourish, achieve success—but in a detached manner. By trying to balance all aspects of life,

During his first tour of America and Canada with Pandit Ravi Shankar, 1968.

we gradually lost our value system and totally disconnected with nature. We are trapped in the wrong type of education system and the values that we got from our parents are missing today because parents are working and do not have time for their children. The focus within society has changed. But I found one place that was different—Sathya Sai Baba's ashram, where value-based education is still being given. Baba used to say it is educare, not education. Your thinking should not be based on getting results at whatever cost, by undercutting or harming others. This whole process has polluted all minds. And, as a result, whether it is politics, or any profession—doctors, musicians—we want shortcuts and that too in the shortest possible time to gain the maximum materialistic achievement, not holistic achievement. You are just thinking about I, me, myself, not about the other person.

Materialism is not bad. Everybody deserves a good house, to have good food, enjoy life. That's not bad. But our soul is dead because our values have deteriorated and now there are no values.

IP: When you first moved into your own house, you saw the mountains in the distance. And today, there are buildings everywhere. Yet, you said, look on the other side and there is a tree ...

SKS: Yes, I don't look at that side. I look this side. The trees are there.

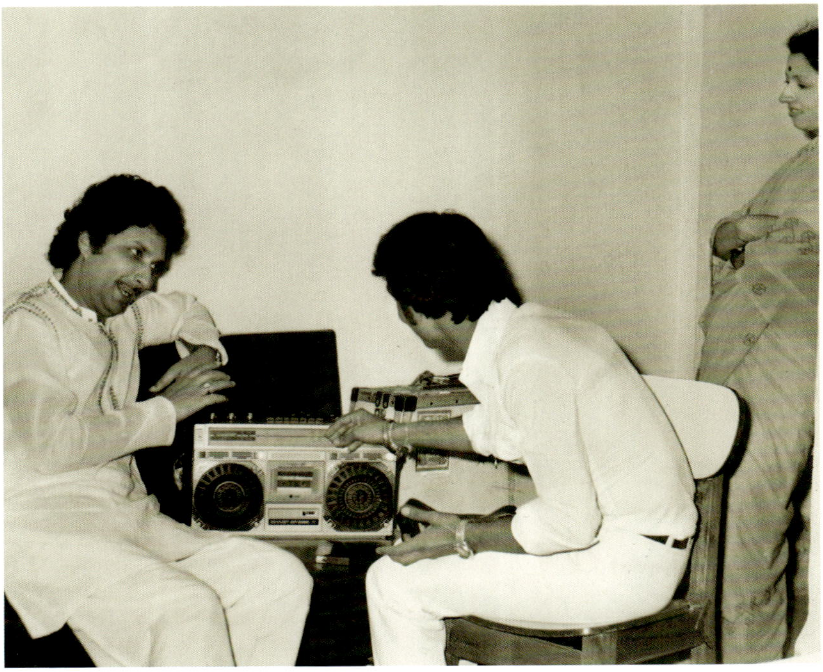

Listening to the recording of a concert at a friend's house in Sholapur.

Top and above: Celebrating Rohit's birthday with family and friends.

Clockwise from right: Cutting the cake at Rohit's birthday; With Rohit, Rahul and their friends in the garden; With young Rahul at home.

IP: Where your own family is concerned—your sons, their wives and your granddaughter—you have taken care to make them imbibe values, which is a kind of personal gift from you. And for this I think your wife, Manoramaji, is equally responsible.

SKS: She is greatly responsible because she took care of the kids while I pursued my music. This would not have been possible without her help. And I'm very happy and satisfied with what

my sons, Rohit and Rahul, have achieved, which they have done on their own merit. I have always encouraged them in my role as their father. As I said, each individual soul brings different *sanskara*. Rohit and Rahul are different individuals with different abilities. I have consciously tried never to impose my thoughts or choices on them; I never forced my ideas. Although Rahul is in the same profession, I'm very glad that at one point in time, he himself told me, 'Papa, I no more want to play duets with you. People should know me for what I am and for what I can do on my own.' He added, 'I know I will lose many concerts and I will not get that much money, but I'm ready to face it.' I was very happy.

With Pandit Hariprasad Chaurasia, Girija Devi and friends.

Christmas at the White House, Washington, during a tour of the US, 1974.

Rahul is a very good composer, he is very gifted. He has even tried out something which I have never done. I thought that the combination of the santoor and the saxophone is wrong. I was offered a concert with a well-known saxophone player from Norway, which I did not accept. When Rahul planned to play with Kenny G, the best-known saxophonist in the world, I did not object because I believe that we should let our children do what they are doing. Let them experience life on their own and make their own mistakes. They will learn better from their mistakes rather than from our imposed ideas. And I'm seeing the results. When I heard Rahul and Kenny G's album, I had

to change my opinion about the santoor and the saxophone being played together. I have always been very open with my kids. And when they face some difficulty, a problem or failure, then they learn from that. I think this is how I have learned.

IP: I remember your first concert with Rahul in Kolkata many years ago. And Rahul was also interested in the cricket match that was being played at that time. But, when the concert hour approached, he was very serious and totally focussed. I saw in you a kind of tranquillity, which seemed to me strange and odd because you were not nervous. This is Kolkata where you have achieved great success, you have a huge fan following there. You've been playing there for years, given your own past association with the city. But you were very, very relaxed. And when the concert started at Birla Sabha Gharit, it just had its own moments of magic. There was no stress and no tension from your side.

Top: Playing before a Kashmiri Sufi saint at music director Naushad's residence, 1961-62. Above: At a concert with Ustad Allarakha and Ustad Sabir Khan, conducted by Pandit Ravi Shankar, in the US, 1968.

Top: At a concert in Mumbai with Pandit Kishen Maharaj on the tabla, 1966.
Above: With Pandit Hariprasad Chaurasia in the US, 1971.

Temperamentally, Shivji and I were very different. He was an introvert while I loved the company of family and friends. In those early days, new to Mumbai and marriage, I would try and draw him out, willing him to spend more time with me but soon I realised that no matter how much he cared about me, Shivji's first love would always be his music.

Manorama Sharma

SKS: That was a very big risk I took, it could have gone the other way also.

IP: Exactly.

SKS: Because immediately people compare. When they're hearing it one by one, one after another, they compare the tonal quality, they compare the musicality, they compare everything. So I took that risk because I had that confidence in Rahul.

IP: Do you regret not playing with your father like you played with Rahul?

With wife Manorama and son Rahul at home.

SKS: My father never played the santoor. That's another very interesting thing because he was a vocalist, but that chance never came that he sang and I played the santoor.

IP: Or the tabla?

SKS: I played the tabla with him at home as well as in some concerts.

IP: Coming back to the time you played with Rahul—I remember it was quite spectacular. After that he has taken off on his own, also as a composer where he has formed his own iconography, his own language, which is very distinctive and completely individualistic. He could be, in a way, inspired. His film music may have certain inspiration from you, but it's totally original in its timbre and texture. There is nothing there but Rahul Sharma himself, which is a great achievement.

SKS: You see why I am satisfied and wherever my father's soul is, he must be happy, too. He gave me this instrument and nobody knew at that point in time what is going to happen with it, although he was very sure. But then my biggest worry was that the instrument, the santoor, should not end with me, and because of that, I started teaching. Normally musicians are very strict in selecting their disciples. They judge them and then choose those who have got the ability, are dedicated and many other factors. I just relaxed these factors thinking that, perhaps, some of them might pick up the skill along the way. Besides, I strongly believe and history also tells us that no musician can give you ten disciples of the same calibre. Baba Allaudin Khan was an exception—Ustad Ali Akbar Khan, Pandit Ravi Shankar, Pandit Nikhil Banerjee, Annapurna Devi were all his *shishyas* and each is brilliant in his or her right. Otherwise, you will not find a guru giving you so many disciples of that calibre. Normally, it is one or rarely two. So I taught many students, but some of them did not come on the stage at the right time because of family circumstances and other factors. I was once really worried, and so were my listeners, as to the future of the santoor. But today, I'm happy that the santoor will live on.

Facing page: Being felicitated after playing a duet with Pandit Hariprasad Chaurasia in the early sixties.

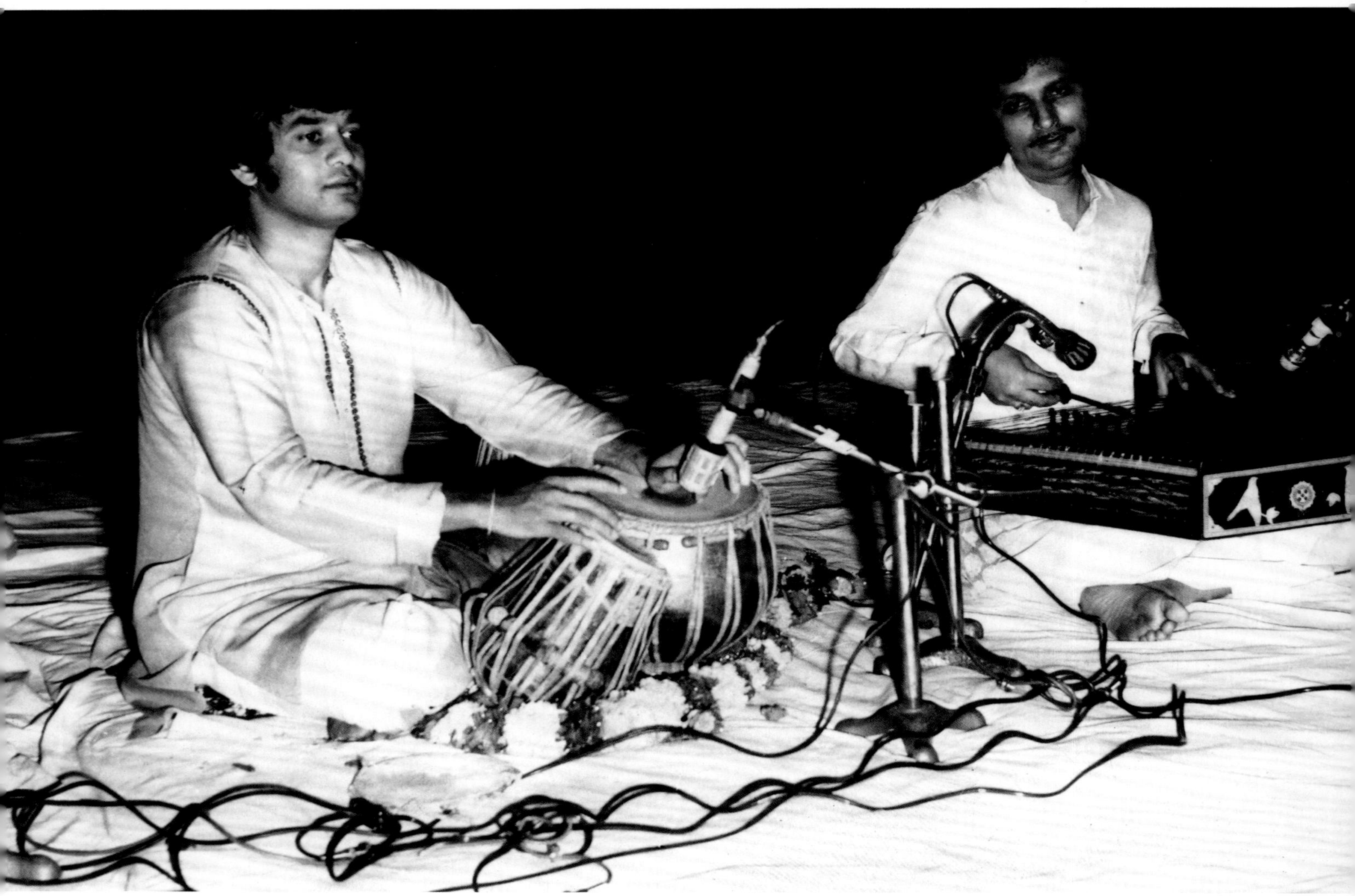

IP: Of course.

SKS: Rahul has fulfilled that promise, which I wanted in a disciple, the promise of not only being a clone of Shiv Kumar Sharma, to have the ability to present my music the way it is, but to add something of his own in it. With the grace of God, he has achieved just that. And now, I hear from my listeners that they're also happy. Rahul has gone through the entire learning process and has been accepted. Ultimately, I feel, listeners will accept the musician if he has the ability. I reiterate, if the musician has

'My own development as a tabla player owes so much to Shivji. I saw melody and rhythm come together in a way that had never happened on stage before!'
Ustad Zakir Hussain

After a concert in Karwar, with Mohan Hemmadi, Pandit Hariprasad Chaurasia and Swamiji (centre).

got the ability, people might take time to accept his/her music, but they will accept it eventually. Unfortunately, a materialistic attitude has crept into our profession, which is called a spiritual profession. Musicians are trying out shortcuts by different means in order to be in the news and to promote themselves. I think this is not the right path to reach your destination. The right path is to do your work sincerely and prove yourself every day, in every concert. It's not like once you get a degree or a PhD, then for life you're given a job and after that a pension.

This profession is not like that. You have to prove yourself every day and keep learning and adding something different to your music. Now, for instance, Rahul has been playing for sixteen years professionally. That is quite a long period to prove yourself.

IP: And he has won laurels. He's been successful as a musician.

SKS: Now, right now, he is not inclined to teach, which is a cause of worry for me. But maybe later because then it should go to the next generation.

'Shivji is a musician who is equally good at melody and rhythm (being an erstwhile tabla player).'
Ustad Zakir Hussain

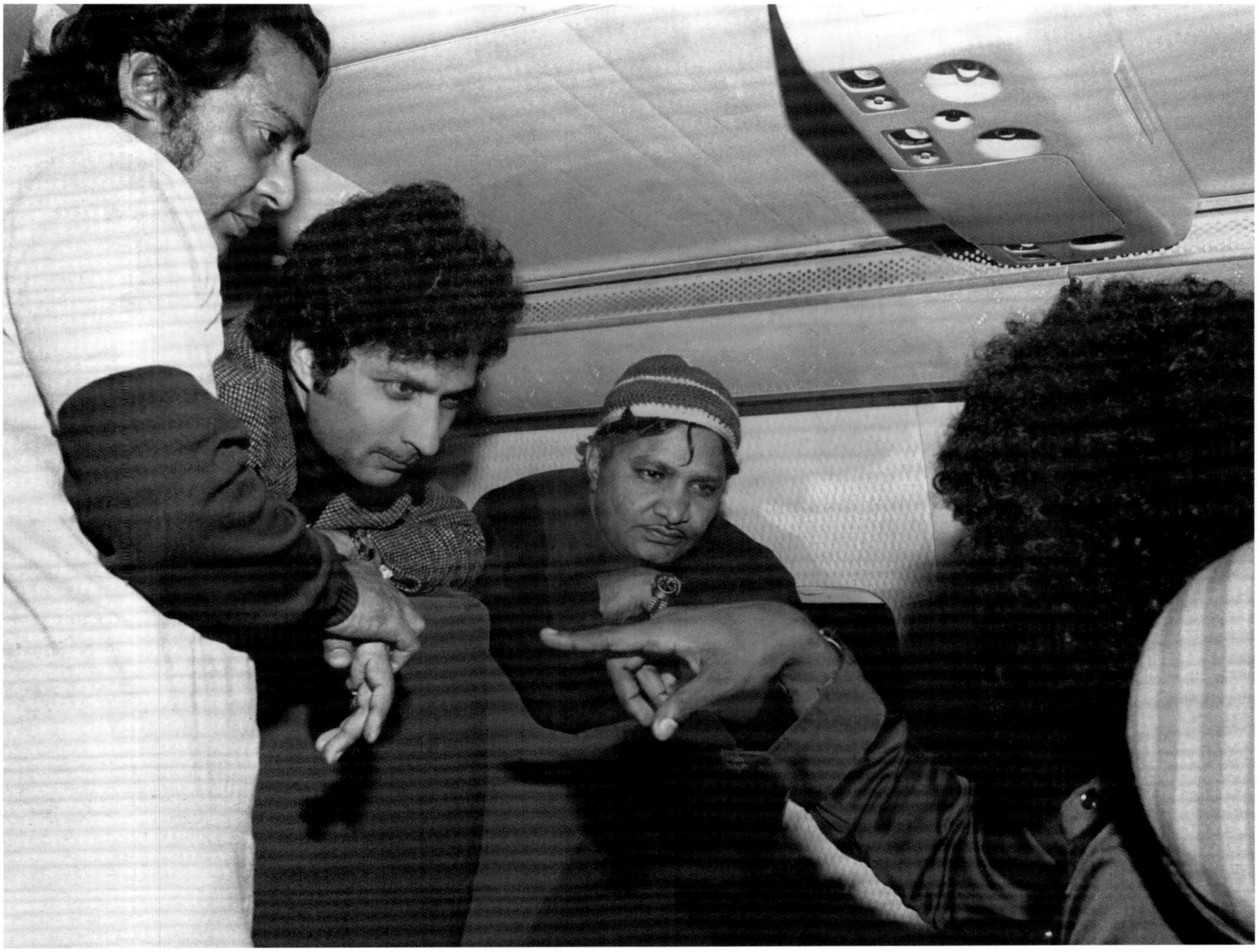

In a chartered plane with Kartick Kumar, Pandit Hariprasad Chaurasia and Billy Preston (back to camera).

IP: How did you feel when you won the Padma Shri and later the Padma Vibhushan?

SKS: It's an honour.

IP: You have had such disagreements with All India Radio about your designated place in the ratings.

SKS: Yes, they were adamant and so was I till I won my place in the end! The awards—the Padma Shri first and then the Padma Vibhushan—are a recognition of that instrument which some

Top: With Toni (wife of Zakir Hussain), Pandit Hariprasad Chaurasia and Ustad Zakir Hussain.
Above: Offering prayers at the mausoleum of a Sufi saint in Nagpur.

AVINASH PASRICHA

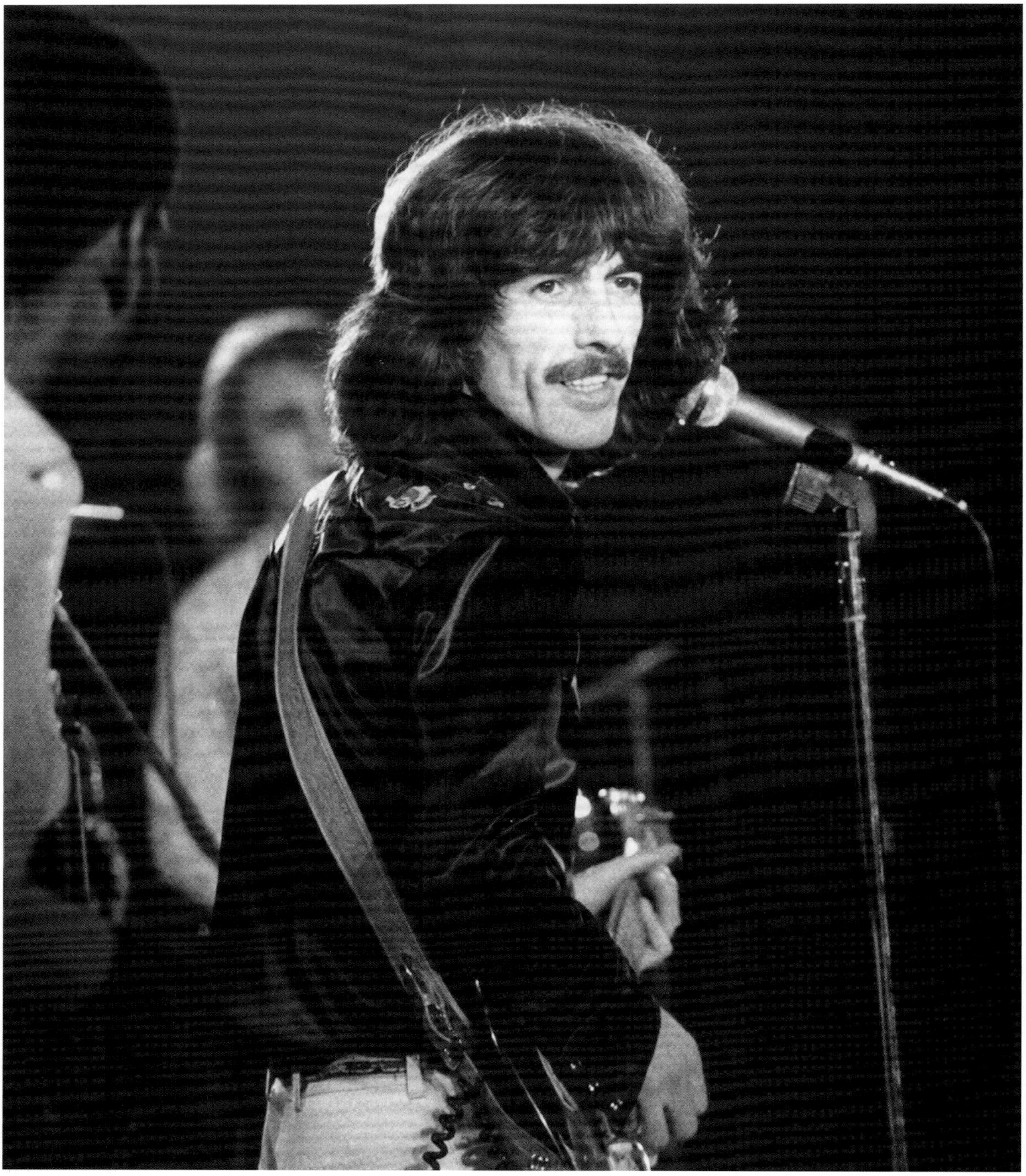

Superstar George Harrison, who was part of the grand tour in 1968.

In Europe with Ustad Zakir Hussain, in the seventies.

people had initially criticised and discarded. So there was satisfaction from that point of view. Recently, I played in the central hall of Parliament House on the occasion of the sixtieth anniversary of Parliament. The President, Prime Minister and parliamentarians were present. I shared a coincidence in my life with that particular day. The coincidence is, they were celebrating sixty years of the Parliament of India and it was sixty years of the santoor's journey as a concert instrument.

In the green room in Philadelphia with Ustad Zakir Hussain, tuning the tanpura. Looking on is tanpura player Ameera.

With Pandit Hariprasad Chaurasia, Peter Sellers and his friend, Ustad Sultan Khan and Kartick Kumar, during the tour of the US, 1974.

IP: If it is a valediction, it validates everything. And then you played at the august Nobel Prize function?

SKS: Yes, Hariji (Hariprasad Chaurasia) and I were the first Indian musicians to perform there. But for me now, it is just a date, a day. I played in an engineering college and I asked the students to close their eyes and listen to the music and after I finish, to keep their eyes closed until I tell them to open them. I then asked a student what he had felt. His reply, 'I felt I was there

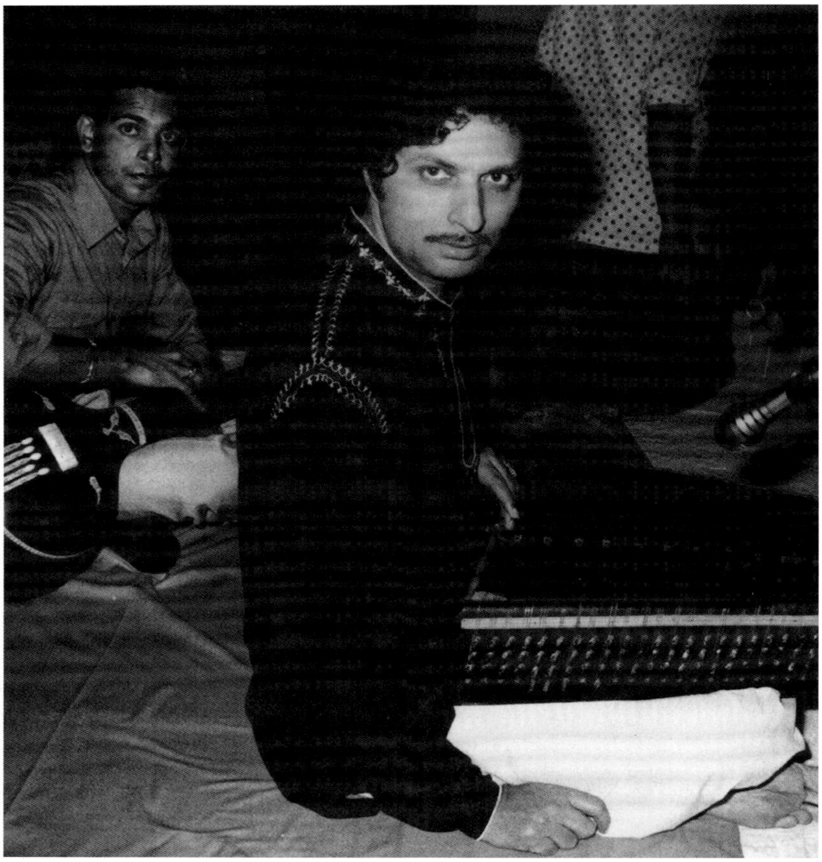

Sound-check at an early concert.

and God was there and nothing else was there.' This kind of reaction is more important for me than getting a doctorate, or other awards, or even a fellowship of Sangeet Natak Akademi. My music is different today than what I was playing some ten years ago. I'm not playing that kind of speed now. A musician cannot maintain the speed of music after a while but we don't accept that. We don't want to accept it. I will play my music till the day I feel I am doing justice to this instrument. The day I feel, because of my age or any other factor, that I am not doing justice to my music, I'll give up playing in public. I am looking at different avenues to find what I can do. I can take people on this journey where I can try to make them be one with me and experience something different. I tried this at the Womad festival in Australia and New Zealand. This festival is held in big

A rare photograph from the tour, Pandit Ravi Shankar, Peter Sellers and George Harrison in front of their private aircraft.

Receiving the Padma Vibhushan from President KR Narayanan.

Shivji taught me to discipline my energies—he made me do *riyaz*, attend classical music concerts and devote my hours to perfecting the bansuri. He made me understand the futility of wasting time in trivial pursuits when the Indian classical scene was primarily dominated by the sitar, sarod and shehnai. He made me realise the urgency of staking our claim at this critical juncture. He has been like an elder brother to me and our friendship has given me strength.

Pandit Hariprasad Chaurasia

After a concert in Paris with his wife Manorama, Pandit Hariprasad Chaurasia and Ustad Shafaat Ahmed Khan.

Top: With student Adnan Sami after a concert in Mumbai.
Above: With Yash Chopra, Nusrat Fateh Ali Khan and Ustad Shafaat Ahmed Khan.

DAYANITA SINGH

DAYANITA SINGH

Top: At Karwar beach during the Sangeet Research Academy tours.
Above: With Pandit VG Jog during the Sangeet Research Academy tours.

AVINASH PASRICHA

At Rashtrapati Bhawan after the release of Journey with a Hundred Strings: My Life in Music. *Seen in the picture (from L to R) are Ravi Puri, VS Ailawadi, Arti Ailawadi, David Davidar (behind), Manorama, former President of India Abdul Kalam, Pandit Shiv Kumar Sharma, Manjit Bawa and Ina Puri.*

parks, they have different tents, with different kinds of music. Somewhere rock music is going on, at another place jazz music and at yet another place I am playing one instrument with one tabla. In the western world, music is known as entertainment. I said, I call it beyond entertainment. And I told them the same thing which I had tried at the engineering college in Pune. I asked them to close their eyes, 'Don't think about what I'm playing and where this music is from. It is just a sound. And I'm trying to take you inward.' So this is my focus now, I'm trying that. I'm enjoying the moment. The reaction I'm getting from people, even from the western listeners, is encouraging. They tell me that they experience so much joy while hearing my music, it is as if a spark is ignited within, thereby illuminating their souls.

DAYANITA SINGH

Sangeet Research Academy tour with Pandit Vijay Kichlu.

Such a Long Journey

Rare photographs from the albums of the Sangeet Research Academy and personal archives

N SAMIRAN

DAYANITA SINGH

On and off stage, with Ustad Zakir Hussain.

DAYANITA SINGH

DAYANITA SINGH

DAYANITA SINGH

'The contribution of the Sangeet Research Academy towards the promotion of Indian classical music was invaluable and involved the participation of gurus and *shishya*s in the tours across the country, where concerts were sometimes even held under the open skies. Often in attendance were luminaries such as Ravi Shankar, Vilayat Khan, Kishori Amonkar, Balamuralikrishna, Kishan Maharaj, Allarakha, Sitara Devi, Girija Devi, Rajan and Sajan Mishra. SRA scholars such as Ajay Chakraborty and Rashid Khan also performed there; they went on to become brilliant maestros themselves.' ***Pandit Shiv Kumar Sharma***

Clockwise from top left: With Pandit Bhimsen Joshi and Pandit Hariprasad Chaurasia; With Ustad Allarakha; Ustad Ali Akbar Khan's puja room.

RATHCEL STUDIO, JODHPUR

RATHCEL STUDIO, JODHPUR

At the Jodhpur palace.

Above: With Pandit VG Jog.
Facing page: With Ustad Amjad Ali Khan.

His deep understanding of the santoor has revolutionalised the music world.

Shivji's Tryst with the Santoor

Vijay Kichlu

In a lighter moment at the Sangeet Research Academy, Kolkata, with Pandit Vijay Kichlu.

In the fifty years that I have known Pandit Shiv Kumar Sharma, who is lovingly addressed as Shivji, I must have witnessed at least two hundred of his recitals and each time it has been more or less the same experience. Curtain opens—he enters, sits on the dais with folded hands, looks around at his audience with a confident smile and the whispers start: 'Wow! How handsome!', 'What a personality' and so on. Very few people know that Shivji is certainly impressive but not just externally. His internal strength—spiritual, intellectual and emotional—has revolutionalised the music world.

Radio concert in Jammu with sitar player Ilyas Khan of Lucknow.

Until about sixty or seventy years ago, the santoor was hardly known to anyone connected with Indian classical music, even though musicologists trace its origin to centuries ago when a string instrument called the shata-tantri veena, or veena with hundred strings, was in existence. Later, somehow the santoor got popular only in Kashmir and for centuries has been used there mostly as an accompanying instrument for vocalists singing Sufiana Mausiqi or music related to the Sufi philosophy. Occasionally, the santoor is still used as a solo instrument in Kashmir but only to play Sufi music. The word santoor, derived from Persian, also means a hundred strings.

Instruments similar to the santoor are found in different parts of the world but with different names. In China it is called yang quin, in Germany hackbret, in Greece santoori, in Hungary cymbalom and in Iran and Iraq it is known as the santoor. In all these countries the instrument has got around one hundred strings and, it is only in the

An informal mehfil *with tabla player Pandit Anokhelal, Pandit VG Jog and Pandit Lalmani Mishra.*

With Pandit Hariprasad Chaurasia and Pandit Ravi Shankar.

valley of Kashmir that it has exactly a hundred strings. This fact also establishes the link of the Kashmiri santoor to the shata-tantri veena. It is quite possible that the instrument got its present name, santoor, because of the Persian influence in India during the twelfth or thirteenth centuries. Some musicologists, however, do maintain that the santoor originated in Iran. Indian musicologists and some ancient music sculptures establish that it is an ancient Indian instrument. Perhaps gypsies travelling from India to Europe and other parts of the world carried this instrument with them and it was adopted by some of those countries with a different name and shape.

According to our ancient peers, instruments can be classified in four categories—*tata* or string instruments such as the sarod and the sitar; *susira* or hole instruments such as the flute and the shehnai; *avanaddha* or instruments covered with skin such as the mridangam and the tabla and *ghana* or instruments made of brass or wood to mark time. These classifications are regarded as, perhaps, the soundest by western musicologists as well. The santoor does not strictly fall into any of these four categories. This is because when playing any string instrument, the fingers of at least one hand touch the strings, as experienced while playing the sitar, sarod or violin. However, the santoor is played with mallets or *kalam* which strike the strings and the musician's fingers do not touch any string except as part of innovation.

Shivji is the son and disciple of the late Pandit Uma Dutt Sharma, who belonged to a family of priests and later turned into a musician. He lived in Jammu and was trained by the legendary musician Pandit Bade Ramdasji, one of the all-time greats of the Banaras *gharana*. Pandit Uma Dutt Sharma was not only a learned vocalist but also an accomplished tabla, harmonium and esraj player. In the early fifties he was the music-in-charge of Radio Srinagar. It was during this period that he did extensive research on the santoor and started teaching his son, Shivji, the intricacies of the instrument, particularly in relation to Indian classical music. He taught classical music to Dr Karan Singh, the ex-Maharaja of Kashmir, as well. Shivji was introduced to music at the tender age of five. He was first taught vocal

The HMV Studio, Mumbai, 1967. During the recording session of Call of the Valley *with Pandit Brij Bhushan Kabra (guitar), Pandit Hariprasad Chaurasia (flute) and Pandit Manikrao Popatkar (tabla).*

By God's grace, Shivji has become a much sought after superstar himself. His poise, grace and dignity make him a true musician and a gentleman. In the history of Indian music he will always be mentioned as a pioneer in elevating the santoor to the height of classical refinement. My admiration and blessings are always with him.

Pandit Ravi Shankar

Pandit Ravi Shankar with Lakshmi Shankar before a performance.

With Ustad Allarakha at a concert in the US, 1968.

music, then the tabla and finally the santoor. His performing career started as a tabla player, broadcasting from Jammu and Srinagar radio stations. Few people know that in his early days Shivji provided tabla accompaniment to musicians of the calibre of Pandit Ravi Shankar, Ustad Nisar Hussain Khan, Ustad Abdul Halim Jaffer Khan, Hirabai Barodekar, Begum Akhtar and Siddheshwari Devi. Around 1961, he also provided the tabla accompaniment in a *jugalbandi* with Pandit Ravi Shankar and Ustad Ali Akbar Khan.

While Shivji devoted his life to music, he did not neglect academics and studied for a Master's degree in Economics from the Jammu & Kashmir University. Given the kind of intellectual and spiritual background he came from, it is not surprising that he finally decided to accept the challenge of playing the santoor as his main instrument. To him goes the credit of converting the santoor to one of the major instruments of Indian classical music. Till then only the sitar, the sarod, the shehnai, the flute and the violin were considered major instruments, with the sarangi being used mostly as an accompanying instrument to vocalists. The santoor had many limitations such as striking the strings with mallets only and not with fingers. This made it difficult to produce the vital effects of the important *kriya*s (actions) of classical music such as *meend* (a glide) and *gamak* (a kind of musical jerk). Shivji experimented on the santoor for years in order to enhance its tonal quality and its string arrangement with a view to improving its playing techniques, but without interfering with the inherent character of the instrument and maintaining the conventional techniques of playing.

In Kashmir, musicians keep the santoor on a wooden stand in front of them while playing it. This gives an extra resonance, which is often disturbing. Shivji was the first musician to keep the santoor on his lap while playing and this helped to eliminate the resonance. Placing a weight of eight kilograms on the lap is not easy. Further, it has to be played for hours at a time. Indulging in delicate intricacies and skills with perfection needs an extraordinary strength of posture as well. To achieve this, Shivji had to turn a yogi not only in terms of physical *asana*s (postures in yoga) but in meditation as well. Till today he practices yoga in its purest form. His gait, his sitting posture, in fact his total personality is ample evidence of the fact that he is not only

At a concert in Bhopal.

an extraordinary musician but also a yogi. He is an extremely honest person; a fact acknowledged by all those who have came in contact with him, including impresarios and music organisers. Shivji is responsible for having changed the string arrangement of the santoor by using thirty-one bridges instead of twenty-five and reducing the total number of strings from hundred to ninety-one. The modified

Pandit Shiv Kumar Sharma and Ustad Zakir Hussain soon became household names in the West and were much sought after. Seen here with Naina Shah, a friend.

santoor was thus able to get three clear octaves and chromatic tuning. He insisted that two mallets must be held in the conventional and particular manner, between the trigger and the middle fingers. Any other way of holding the *kalam* would interfere with the instrument's desired tonal quality. With this, he changed the history of the santoor, its stature, its appeal and attraction to music lovers. He was also able to change the instrument's emotional and spiritual expression, which gave the santoor a new identity.

His All India Radio broadcasts of the santoor from Jammu and Srinagar stations in 1952 demonstrated authentic Raga Sangeet. In 1955, Shivji was invited for a performance by the Hari Das Sangeet Sammelan, a major music conference held in Mumbai. A year later, he was invited by Lala Babu's famous All India Music Conference in Kolkata. For this presentation, Shivji was accompanied on the tabla by the legendary Pandit Anokhe Lal of the Banaras *gharana*. His recitals created a tremendous impression and since then he never looked back. Today, there is no well-known music platform, in India or abroad, where Shivji has not been included. All the major international music festivals in the world have invited him and given him the highest honour and position. Shivji's music career has been dominated by a galaxy of instrumental wizards such as Pandit Ravi Shankar, Ustad Ali Akbar Khan, Ustad Vilayat Khan, Ustad Bismillah Khan, Ustad Amjad Ali Khan, Pandit VG Jog and Pandit Hariprasad Chaurasia. Once during a public performance, where several musicians were present and so was I, the legendary Ustad Vilayat Khan announced, '*Isme koi shak nahi ki hum sab ne bohut naam kamaya par yeh manana parega ki hamare sab ke peechhey to pushton ki tawareekh hai par Shivji ne apne hi dam par santoor jaise saaz ko mausiqui ki duniyan mein khara kar diya, yeh bohut bari baat hai! Is liye Shivji ka aur Bismillah Khan Saheb ka makam hum se alag hai.*' (There is no doubt that we have earned a great name for ourselves but we have to accept that we all had the support of our ancestors who passed on the knowledge to us, but Shivji established an instrument like the santoor in the world of classical music entirely on his own. It is a great achievement and, therefore, both Shivji and Bismillah Khan Saheb occupy a different position.)

Accompanying Hirabai Barodekar at a concert organised by Jammu Radio, 1956-57.

With close friend Girdhari Kaul at his Jammu residence in the fifties.

As a music critic, I am amazed at Shivji's genius in raising himself to the status of the highest grade of musicians of his times. He did not have the benefit of learning the traditional *gat*s (fixed compositions) of the santoor since the santoor had no history of classical music. With his background of vocal music, he composed *gat*s of extraordinary excellence, with a melodic and rhythmic blend. Indeed, some of his *gat*s are mind-boggling as far as rhythmic

With Pandit Vijay Kichlu after a concert.

movements are concerned. His knowledge of the tabla is also amazing and it has helped him in structuring his entire *baaj*. All the tabla maestros agree that they are at their best when accompanying Shivji in any performance. Some of his performances with the phenomenal tabla wizard Ustad Zakir Hussain have been stunning and have left audiences frozen with ecstasy.

Shivji's *ragdari* (classical composition) is immaculate and to the best of my knowledge has never been adversely commented upon by any musician or music critic. By and large it has been authentic and non-controversial. His repertoire of ragas used in public has not been large; generally about twenty-five to thirty, but that does not necessarily mean that his knowledge is confined to just thirty ragas. The late Bharat Ratna Pandit Bhimsen Joshi used just about twenty ragas or so for his public performances and yet he has been accepted as one of the greatest vocalists that India has produced. Owing to the inherent character of an instrument such as the santoor, many ragas with their own specific character and movements are not suitable to play on it. Further, with the quality of *layakari* (different rhythmic patterns) Shivji indulges in, its distribution does not always suit the melodic

Above and left: At an informal session at home in Mumbai with his wife Manorama and Ustad Zakir Hussain in the seventies.

structure and movements of some ragas. In any case, these days even those musicians who possess a sound knowledge of a few hundred ragas use only a selected few for public performances. This, perhaps, suits the taste of the audience. Sixty or seventy years ago, musicians used *aprachalit* or rare ragas freely when *mehfil*s (gatherings) were in vogue and they had to perform before a knowledgeable audience.

The creative genius of a musician is put to test when he/she has to elaborate on a raga with perfect understanding and execution of its

Right: During a rehearsal in Jammu, early 1950.
Below: At a felicitation with Pandit VG Jog, Ustad Zakir Hussain and others.

Enthralling the western music lovers. George Harrison's iconic insignia, 'The Dark Horse' flutters above.

nuances, keeping in mind the constraints of its melodic structure and the rules of the *chalan* (movements). And this has to be done with attractive skills together with the utmost aesthetic appeal. The human voice can execute these nuances fluently but for instrumentalists the make and the character of the instrument can be a restriction. While for the sarod, the fingers move on the strings horizontally, for the violin and the sarangi they move vertically and as such there is no technical difficulty in producing attractive *meend*s and *gamak*s if the musician possesses the ability to do so. For the sitar the fingers move on the strings both vertically and horizontally and both *meend*s and *gamak*s are freely executed. But for the santoor and the jaltarang, it

In the green room after a concert with Sitara Devi, Pandit Birju Maharaj and others.

Top: After a concert with Durga Jasraj, Adnan Sami, Fazal Qureshi and Manorama.
Above: At Ustad Ali Akbar Khan's residence in San Francisco along with Ustad Shafaat Ahmed Khan in the nineties.

Speaking during a felicitation. Gana Saraswati Kishori Amonkar is sitting next to him.

is not possible to use these important *kriya*s. Shivji decided that he would not interfere with the conventional technique of playing his instrument. His imagination led him to find a way of handling the important nuance, the *meend*, by sliding the mallets on the strings delicately in such a manner that it would create the effect of a *meend* without touching the strings with his fingers. This and many other shortcomings of the instrument were covered by his marvellous rhythmic management. His creative excellence certainly finds a better expression when he plays *dhun*s (tunes) as concluding pieces of his recitals.

Shivji, along with Pandit Hariprasad Chaurasia, has acted as a music director for at least eight mainstream films. Their first film *Silsila* was an instant hit and earned the highest distinction of a Platinum Disc, with some of the songs still featuring in the 'haunting' category. Classical musicians, who have also been film music directors, are often pressed by their audience to play popular film songs, a request to which they sometimes succumb. But, to the best of my knowledge, there has not been a single occasion when Shivji has surrendered to such public demands as he has kept his classical music appearances strictly and purely classical.

Facing page: With Kishori Amonkar after her felicitation. Right: With Dr Balamuralikrishna after a concert.

At Pandit Shiv Kumar Sharma's sixtieth birthday celebrations, with Ustad Amjad Ali Khan, Pandit Jasraj, Ustad Allarakha, Pandit CR Vyas, Pandit Hariprasad Chaurasia, Ustad Abdul Halim Jaffer Khan and Ustad Zakir Hussain.

|| जीवेत शरदः शतम् ||
htyabdipoorti Samaroh ||
DIT SHIVKUMAR SHARMA

Sharing a light moment with Pandit Jasraj.

Music is not just notes or rhythmic patterns. A musician cannot establish the spirit of a raga just by knowing its notes, which are like a skeleton, or knowing even its specific movements or *chalan*. He/she has to enter the interior, the feeling, or the *rasa* of the raga, awaken it and bring it to life. Similarly, a musician cannot be judged just by the visual impressions he/she creates, the personality he/she possesses or the skills and acrobatics that impact a listener's mind. It is important to go deeper to understand his/her interior. Listening to Shivji playing the santoor is like listening to his emotions, his vibrations to you. It does not appear for a moment as if he is indulging in any academic exercise. We can enjoy his music even without knowing its language.

With long-time tabla companion Ustad Shafaat Ahmed Khan, 1998.

Shivji brought the santoor to the classical music platform in the mid-fifties. What a sense of fulfilment it must be to him that during his lifetime, and while he is still at his peak, the santoor has become one of the popular instruments of Indian classical music, with several young santoor performers demonstrating their skills. As for Shivji, he has not only attained the highest stature, love, respect and admiration from millions of music lovers and followers all over the world but the Government of India has also recognised his services and has awarded him the second highest civilian award, the Padma Vibhushan.

Every great musician's responsibility, in my opinion, should not end at being a distinguished and a popular musician. He/she must produce at least one worthy disciple during his lifetime—one who can carry forward the tradition and the legacy of the guru. By worthy disciple I mean that disciple who is competent enough to occupy the throne of his guru. Shivji has not just been a musician par excellence, like many other distinguished musicians of his time, but he has also discharged

In Japan after a concert. Seated next to Pandit Shiv Kumar Sharma is Ustad Shafaat Ahmed Khan and standing (from L to R) are two Japanese students, Miyan Shita and Rahul.

his role as a guru admirably. His disciples love and worship him. Quite a few have made a name for themselves and are performing domestically and internationally. Many who have trained abroad have also attained high standards of musicianship. These include Harjinderpal Singh and Kiranpal Singh from England, Nandu Mule now living in the US and Miyan Shita and Taka Hiro from Japan. Besides these disciples, there is Shivji's son, Rahul, whom Shivji has trained admirably in the true *guru-shishya-parampara* (succession from guru to disciple tradition). This he has been able to achieve because Rahul is his son and lives with him. I have no doubt in my

Shiv has deeply impressed me with his deep and scholarly approach towards music. He has proven to the world that the santoor is irrevocably a part of Indian classical music.

Ustad Vilayat Khan

In the green room with Ustad Vilayat Khan, Satish Vyas and Ustad Shafaat Ahmed Khan.

At an award function in Mumbai with former President, Dr Abdul Kalam, Pandit Jasraj and Jagjit Singh.

Top: Presenting a cheque to Prime Minister Dr Manmohan Singh.
Above: After a santoor jugalbandi *with Rahul and Ustad Zakir Hussain in Mumbai, 1998.*

At Sathya Sai Baba's ashram as a devotee.

mind that Rahul is one of the most, if not the most, outstanding young musician of our time and is on his way to becoming truly entitled to occupy the *gaddi* (seat) of his father. Shivji allowed Rahul to develop and expand his creativity and to experiment with his music in various genres—classical to folk, to new age and world fusion. Rahul, on his part, has attained rare distinctions in new creative fields apart from classical music. He has released more than fifty live and studio recordings. Some of Rahul's recent works are his live recordings with the tabla percussion wizard Ustad Zakir Hussain, which are sensational. In 2002, Rahul became the first Indian musician to record with the highest selling French pianist, Richard Clayderman. He composed two albums with Clayderman called 'Confluence'. Till date, these are probably one of India's highest selling instrumental albums. In 2011, Rahul released another best-selling album called 'Namaste India' with the world-renowned saxophonist Kenny G; the album also features the voice of Amitabh Bachchan. All the compositions were done by Rahul and Kenny G plays live with him.

Shivji's father had said to him, 'I want you to make the santoor your instrument and career.' It seems that he had a premonition about the deep relationship between Shivji and the santoor and his son lived up to his *aadesh* (instructions) by accepting the challenge. Thus destiny gave us a legend in the true sense.

Pandit Shiv Kumar Sharma's association with films began with Jhanak Jhanak Payal Baje, *where he played in the background score. Later, his collaboration with Pandit Hariprasad Chaurasia led to their successful innings in many Yash Chopra films. Shiv-Hari composed music for many hits, including* Silsila.

A Parallel Journey: Composing for Cinema

Manek Premchand

Say you have to make a day visit to South Mumbai's popular residential district, Cuffe Parade. There is a fair chance that if you are into Indian food, you may end up eating at a restaurant called Santoor. Amble along with the rich and famous near the world's grandest avenue, the Champs-Elysees in Paris, and you are likely to stumble upon a restaurant called Santoor. Go to a supermarket in India and in the soaps' area you may find a beauty bar named Santoor. Behind this section, you could discover blades marketed in that name. Pass by a *paan wallah* around the corner, and you will see a *paan masala* product of that name. Why, there is even a Santoor Lounge on Facebook, coming out of Bengaluru, providing many valuable health and beauty tips. These are just some of the many things that are named after the santoor. Fifty years ago, none of these names existed. Now wait, this isn't a new technology product. They are talking about a centuries-old instrument. So why is the world romancing the word so much?

To historically understand how and why this gentle ripple, which turned into a tidal wave, came upon us, ever so unnoticeably, we

With playback singer Mohammad Rafi during a recording session in Mumbai.

At EMI's iconic Abbey Road Studios to remix the music of the film Silsila, *London, 1980.*

have to connect many dots. These dots have to do with the musical instrument, the santoor, its sound, its origins and capabilities, how it is played and so on. That of course, but its success has even more to do with the boy whom destiny identified as just the right musical prodigy, born at just the right time and place. The santoor, referred to in the Vedas as shata-tantri-veena and played for centuries by Sufi musicians in the Kashmir valley, was waiting for a key person to take it out of the valley, and into Jammu at first, some three hundred kilometres south. A young lad in Jammu, his boyhood sizzling up with musical maturity, would be miraculously made the instrument's cultural custodian in the decades to come.

Yes, what else but destiny elected him to help understand the instrument's personality and, over decades of toil, guide it into the hearts of generations of music-lovers, in India and abroad? All this happened not just because of his classical repertoire, but in no small measure also because of the man's engagement with the instrument in Hindi cinema, which when it does, offers such a huge opportunity and recognition platform. The question that implores us to answer

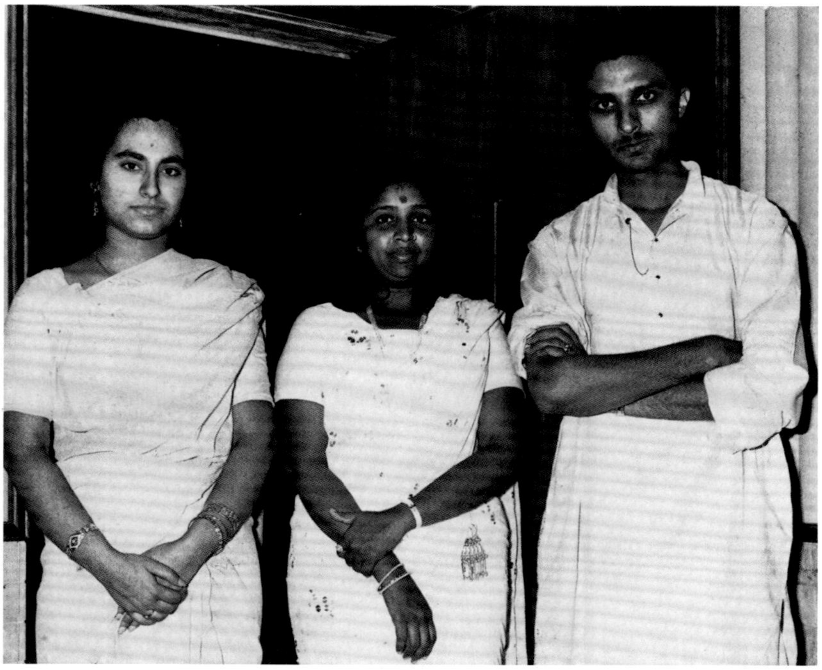

At Rajkamal Studio, Mumbai, with Manorama and Asha Bhonsle, 1966.

Recording for Silsila *at HMV Studio with Ramnarayan, Amitabh Bachchan and Pandit Hariprasad Chaurasia, 1980.*

then is, *who* is this man who has virtually single-handedly, in a lifetime's work of over fifty years, created such an international appeal and acclaim for the santoor and its sound? Let's demystify him, while quickly getting into his film association.

The man we all know as Padma Vibhushan Pandit Shiv Kumar Sharma, with honorary doctorates from several universities today, was hardly just another kid, at least musically. His father Pandit Uma Dutt Sharma was an acclaimed musician and vocalist of the Banaras *gharana*, teaching singing to the likes of a young Karan Singh, in Jammu where he lived and worked as music-in-charge at the radio station. How does the Hindi saying go? *Billi apne bachchon ko ghar-ghar ka rukh dikhaati hai* (A cat shows its children every corner of the house). So of course, little Shiv's training was started in singing and on the tabla. This training happened in the *guru-shishya parampara* way, meaning one-on-one.

In a few months, young Shiv realised that he was quite enjoying playing the tabla. Genetic fortune had given him the start, and innate talent had helped him along; so after extensive *riyaaz* of about two years, he was pretty quickly in the swim of things as far as ragas and *ragini*s went, as also of the patterns of rhythms and so on. He even started giving tabla performances, both on the stage as well as on the radio, when he was only eight years old! He went on giving these performances for some five more years, when something significant happened.

His father, returning for a break during his transfer to Radio Srinagar, brought with him a santoor, and gave it to his perplexed son. Uma Duttji had been doing some study of the instrument and had come to the dream conclusion that since he himself couldn't, it would be his son who would succeed in extracting classical juices out of the santoor, in a Christopher Columbus, 'first-here' kind of way. So, he said, 'Learn to play this, Shiv.'

The young lad didn't like the idea at first. For one, he didn't like the instrument's sound all that much. Moreover, he was enjoying both the singing and the tabla and loving the appreciation, too. So now all that was going to go waste? But what were his options? Uma Duttji was both his father and his guru, and refusing either of them would be insubordination! That's how the reluctant young boy started with this instrument. Gradually, he began enjoying it. He did his own research on the instrument too, but what stands out is the discovery that the santoor was not a folk instrument as was (and is even now) commonly believed; it is an instrument that mostly accompanies Sufi singers in the Kashmir valley, even if sometimes we hear it going solo as well. Outside of the Kashmir valley—and that includes Jammu—it was very rarely heard, much less seen, especially up to the mid-century years.

That is how the musical switch happened to the young prodigy, a switch from rhythm to melody. It may be worth pausing here to consider that the world got no opportunity to hear him go in his third talent—singing, even as his tabla-playing is another story. In tabla-

It was an unforgettable *jugalbandi* that happened impromptu that evening. It was spontaneous music composed unrehearsed, with Shivji, Hariji and Zakir Bhai. I don't know where they were drawing inspiration from, I don't know what it was and I have never heard Shivji play the santoor so beautifully. This went on for hours, well past midnight and when it was all over, we could see not just a physical exhaustion on the part of Shivji, but as though, his very soul had been spent. It was pure magic ...

Amitabh Bachchan

Recording the song Rang barse *from the film* Silsila, *with Yash Chopra, Amitabh Bachchan and Pandit Hariprasad Chaurasia.*

playing, he was heard far and wide, since he did accompany many great vocalists and instrumentalists such as Begum Akhtar, Pandit Ravi Shankar, Ustad Ali Akbar Khan, Siddheshwari Devi, among others. In fact, we will brush with his exceptional tabla-playing in cinema too, in a little while.

Seen from the perspective of a man who fully understands the tabla, consider the fun angle now. As a santoor player, he is always backed by some rhythms, and while he hammers away at the dulcimer, his mind is completely aware of what the rhythm accompanist is doing, while in most cases the reverse is not true: the rhythmist may not understand too much of the santoor's personality. That takes away from it being a level playing field, of course, and it offers Shivji a unique edge too, but does he take that advantage? No! You will never have seen him upstage anyone else. He knows that is one of the best ways to both become untrue to his art, as also to dilute the product.

After a recording session at Mehboob Studio, Mumbai, with Ved Rahi, Pyarelal, Mohammad Rafi and Laxmikant.

AVINASH PASRICHA

This master of the santoor is in fact a student of human nature too and knows he wouldn't have got this far had he taken undue advantage of this special strength that he possesses. In fact, this thinking rubs off on his whole persona, because, just as his santoor 'listens' to the other instruments while speaking its own part, Shivji is as keen a listener in human affairs as he is an interesting speaker. You can see his grey-blue eyes focussing all the time. And then when he speaks, he speaks with art and wisdom. Exactly the same way as when his santoor speaks, the world listens! (The mallet used to strike the santoor's strings is called *kalam*, which means a writing instrument, inspired very likely by the conventional *kalam*s of yore, whose job was to write on paper. The *kalam* here 'writes' music instead.)

Of course we know in parallel about Shivji's personality too, and also how he went about changing the instrument, its shape, the manner in which it sits on you, the way it is played, and more—all that like a perennially-obsessed one-man brigade. Let's consider the extraordinary trajectory of his life and trace his enormous work in Hindi cinema now.

The young man was not yet an adult when he came to play for a concert at Mumbai's Swami Haridas festival, put together by the famous event host Brij Narainji. This was in February 1955. The latter had come to see Dr Karan Singh, who had promised the event organiser to despatch a man from Jammu, with an instrument from Kashmir, the likes of which would not have been seen by anyone in Mumbai before.

At the festival, young Shiv played the santoor impressively, and was he lucky that day! Sitting in the audience was a daughter of the great V Shantaram, a young lady called Madhura, who would go on to become the wife of Pandit Jasraj, also performing at the same event.

The young lady met him: 'I am V Shantaram's daughter. I liked the sound of the santoor and you played very well. During the performance I called up my dad and told him about this new

AVINASH PASRICHA

instrument that I just heard and liked. Dad said, "Call him tomorrow to Rajkamal Studio, let me hear this musician". So do please go meet him tomorrow.'

Now this was a golden opportunity. Films were hot then as they are now. Many people try desperately to find an entry into cinema, which has the muscle to catapult you high. But it is characteristic of Shivji to have declined that offer to 'go to the studios tomorrow'. Characteristic because, in his own words, he has often turned away from things, places and opportunities. '*Main chhodta chala gaya hoon. Madhuraji ko mera kehna ki main kal nahin ja paoonga ek himaakat thi.*' ('That was my stupidity.') Especially when you see what more he told her.

'Now look at my stupidity,' says the maestro. 'I said to the lady, "Sorry, I have to leave for Jammu tomorrow. In about a month, I have my second-year exams at college. For eleven months I don't study. In the twelfth month, I read up my friends' notes and appear for my papers. Let me appear for my exams first." My foolhardiness encouraged me to actually tell her I would be free after a certain date in April, and "if you think you still need me, here is my address, please contact me".'

If we consider at this point what all he has been leaving or declining, we would be running ahead of the story. So we will cross such bridges as and when we reach them. Just now, let's stay with 1955.

In April, the postman knocked at his door in Jammu. He had got a telegram, 'Please come to Rajkamal Studio soonest'.

So now we know how a young Shiv Kumar Sharma came to Mumbai for his first film assignment, in April 1955, before he was even eighteen years old. Of course he wasn't hired yet, since his santoor hadn't been auditioned by the boss yet.

The great V Shantaram now met the young musician from Jammu and heard him play the instrument from Kashmir. After he was impressed, Vasant Desai, finishing Shantaram's *Jhanak Jhanak Payal Baje*, was

From rhythm to melody—Pandit Shiv Kumar Sharma achieved both exceptionally well.

roped in. Neither of them had heard of—much less heard—the santoor, and their synergy of excitement became palpable! But there was an issue now. *Jhanak Jhanak Payal Baje*'s songs were done, even as the background score wasn't ready yet. Composer Vasant Desai suggested to young Shiv if he could compose and play the santoor for a scene in a lake. 'Sure,' said the eager young man. He saw the scene a few times, then readied the tune, and that's how the santoor, and the man behind the santoor, made their first audio 'appearance' in Hindi cinema, in a scene that had Gopi Krishna and Sandhya romancing in a boat.

During a concert in Germany in the nineties.

This scene couldn't have been tailored better for the wonderful sound of the santoor, so fresh to cinema. The serene, idyllic tones of the instrument create just the mood for romance, for time slowing down, washing you with a cool pleasant breeze, so to say. *Jhanak Jhanak* was a colour film, refreshing in those black-and-white dominated days, love was in the air, and the lovers were in a slow-moving boat to nowhere. Everyone who saw that scene, also heard the atmosphere being created, and they loved it. V Shantaram was so impressed with this experience, he called the young man over for a tête-à-tête. He asked the musician what his plans were.

'I have appeared for my exams, Sir. If I pass, I will go on and do my BA,' replied the young man.

'But what after your BA?' asked the filmmaker.

'After my graduation? Why, after that, music of course!'

'So why not now? May I offer you my next film as music composer?'

Pandit Shiv Kumar Sharma introduced strains of Dogri folk music in cinema music.

Music composing, before his eighteenth birthday, and that too from that giant film personality V Shantaram? What better opportunity could a young man wish for? But we are at the second important bridge in young Shiv's life, the 'no-no' kind. 'Sorry,' he told the veteran filmmaker, 'my focus is not on films at the moment. From my father, I am learning an instrument that people are scoffing at. Many people are saying the santoor can't handle classical stuff. They think it is my big folly that I am attempting to square the circle. I have got to go, Shantaramji, it's a different calling.'

So then, after a job so well recorded and received, the young man took a train back to Jammu. (Just for the record, Shantaram's next film was *Toofan Aur Diya* [1956], with music again by Vasant Desai.)

After that, young Shiv decided to pursue his studies (even if in the interesting 11+1 way he had mentioned to Shantaram's daughter!) while persevering with the santoor. He was also giving performances on the stage in various cities within India now. He kept putting his everything into the instrument, which in turn kept rewarding him with its sounds. The bond between the two was growing very strong.

What brought him to Mumbai the next time—a full five years later, was an issue having to do with a nine-to-five job. And here we greet his third major milestone, once again a 'no thanks', declining situation. Radio Jammu offered a job as Music Producer to the young man. But artist that he was, Shiv wasn't thrilled; in fact, he just abhorred this sort of regimentation. He would have given up anything to avoid being forced into any regular time zone. So he kept all job thoughts at bay. About a month passed, when his father asked him what was up, had he decided?

'Yes,' he said, 'I don't want to do a nine-to-five job.'

'Then what do you want to do?'

'I want to do something significant for the santoor.'

With actor Vyjayanthimala Bali after a performance at Rashtrapati Bhawan.

'Then what are you doing here? Find a significant platform.'

'Sure,' he replied, 'I leave day after tomorrow.'

'But where are you headed?'

'I am off to ... Bombay.'

In the rush of this story we must keep in mind that he had detoured not one, but two bridges in quick succession here. A plum job offer, which he declined. And his beloved Jammu, family, the comfort zone, all of which he said farewell to, with an air of finality. Hold that up with a 'retrospectoscope' now, and you think maybe that's why they say Fortune favours the brave.

Pockets lined with five hundred rupees from his father, young Shiv took a train and reached Mumbai on 1 June 1960, a bag of clothes in one hand, a santoor in the other, a dream in his mind and no idea at all where he was going to stay. Touts took him to the cheapest hotel available, at his request; ironically, he was taken to Kashmir Hotel, opposite Metro cinema at Dhobi Talao.

Interesting history follows us now as we digress and fast forward for just a few moments. If you are aware of the story of music composer Naushad, then you may know that he had run away from Lucknow to make music in Mumbai. Financially down and out, he had 'stayed' at a Dadar footpath in his early days in the city. Later, when his *Baiju Bawra* was released, it did a silver jubilee at the very theatre which was opposite the footpath the young émigré had made 'home' one day. 'It had taken me seventeen years to cross that footpath!' the maestro was to recount so often, his humour now coming easy.

With Vyjayanthimala Bali (fourth from left), friends and co-performers after a performance at Rashtrapati Bhawan.

Consider Shivji's own parallel now. Kashmir Hotel stood—and still stands—bang opposite Metro cinema, where his first film *Silsila* was released in 1981! As happens to all of us when we recall private moments, Panditji remembers pausing to reflect on those June 1960 days, at the time of the premiere.

AVINASH PASRICHA

Bringing alive memorable scenes in Hindi cinema with the santoor.

With actor Rekha after receiving the Giants Award, 1991.

But let's sprint back to 1960, when Shivji came to Mumbai, bag in hand, and determination in his head. In the coming months, he would be efficiently received by his own share of ups and downs, including spending some sleepless nights, not so much from worry, but for instance from no fan (the landlord hadn't paid his electricity bill, so it was cut off). On another occasion, for somewhat similar reasons, he found himself, baggage and all, dispossessed of a roof one night! But he coped, and all that shrank to insignificance, only because the mission was big, beyond such trivial things.

In this his second visit to Mumbai, young Shiv set out to meet composers. Naturally, Vasant Desai was the first. That didn't produce results this time, so then the young man from Jammu started his rounds of meeting other people. He met GN Joshi of HMV who had heard his work in *Jhanak Jhanak Payal Baje*. The HMV producer gave him a recording. Soon he got a bit more lucky. For one, he met with sarangi virtuoso Pandit Ram Narain, whose elder brother Pandit Chaturlal was an extraordinary tabla player and had performed with young Shiv in Delhi. Ram Narainji in turn was quite close to Roshan and had been doing amazing work for that composer in so many films of the early 1950s. When Shiv met Roshan, the composer had just then finished the sensational songs for *Barsaat Ki Raat* (released later that year, in 1960), but one song, meant for the time the titles came on, was remaining. Roshan heard what Shiv did with the santoor, and took him aboard for that one number, *Garjat barsat saawan aayo ri*. Voila! In weeks was the santoorist given an audience before another amazing composer, Jaidev. Once again, only the background score and one song remained for this maestro's current assignment, Navketan's *Hum Dono*. But the impressed Jaidev wanted to milk the idea of the santoor, and one song is better than none.

The song was exceptional, a Sahir Ludhianvi product of class, *Dukh aur sukh ke raaste bane hain sabke waaste ... Jahaan mein aisa kaun hai ke jisko gham mila nahin*. In the sombre scene, Sadhana is cheering up her sweetheart Dev Anand and saying, 'Look, you and I are not two different people, we are one! Please share with me all your sorrows.' The song's mood was elevated by the magic of the santoor, weaving through the whole tune and accompanied essentially by the tabla, in a melody that has perhaps no expiry date.

Engrossed in a performance with Pandit Hariprasad Chaurasia. Shiv-Hari's tryst with cinema did not in the least compromise their standing in the world of Indian classical music.

On his sixtieth birthday with Manorama, who was a keen singer and was very supportive of his experiments with cinema.

The background score is vital too, as any significant composer will tell you. Dialogues need to be accompanied by the right instruments, at the right volume and timing of highs and lows, so that the story gets people to stay absorbed. In *Hum Dono*'s narrative of two lookalike Dev Anands in the army, one's wife, Nanda, has given up her husband as dead in battle. At this time, near the denouement of the film, the other Dev shows up and explains to her emotively that her husband is alive and well, even if injured. It's a memorable, moving scene, brought alive by many factors including the playing of the santoor, this time in a non-serene way, to reflect the complex emotions that are being experienced on the screen.

In his search for work, Shiv then continued with his rounds, and even as he did so, other composers began to be influenced by both the sound of the santoor as well as by the word-of-mouth campaign

Enjoying Pandit Rajan-Pandit Sajan Mishra's concert in Mumbai.

coming his way, always the best kind of publicity, since there's no commercial angle to it. He continued to remain committed to his cause. And haven't we heard it said before—from the moment of commitment, nature conspires to help you.

These word-of-mouth recommendations got the young musician enough confidence and finance to be able to rent an apartment on his own. The Kashmir Hotel honeymoon had lasted just weeks and

Shiv Kumar Sharma

is undoubtedly one of the greatest legends in our lifetimes.

We remain indebted to him for giving us such wonderful music.

Pandit Rajan-Pandit Sajan Mishra

now no more 'electrical' shocks for him, the kind of power cuts we saw earlier. Towards this end, he found just the place, in Bandra, a Mumbai suburb, but there was a problem he was told. In fact, there were two problems. First, he was informed that the landlord didn't give his apartment to anyone from films. Second, if you were a bachelor, then no again. Shiv Kumar Sharma was both, and his good looks may have gone against him too, bearing the association many people have of *filmi* folk. But the young musician requested a meeting with the landlord and somehow convinced the latter to make an exception.

Moving into Bandra, pretty close to SD Burman's bungalow called Jet, meant meeting up with the maestro soon, and also then playing for both him and his son, Rahul, quite soon, and it was all beginning to happen for the young santoorist now.

At this point, let's consider the placement of the planets to make it just right for this man. Just as he had been

learning the fundamentals of singing and rhythm, an unexplored melody instrument had come along, to get him to understand the wide music canvas better. In a Darwinian 'natural-selection' way, this happened to a gifted, eager boy, only whom nature considered worthy. Examine further the whole checkerboard of his visiting Mumbai, just at the time when romance in cinema was hotting up, and more and more shoots happening in hill stations and mountains as well as lakes, which the santoor's character is most identified with.

Let's digress to offer a significant analogy here. Many competent music historians consider that there were great singers before Lata Mangeshkar too, but when she entered the recording room, surely there was a paradigm shift. Composers were delighted with what this young girl could do with their tunes, so there was no limit to their creativity now. She gave wings to many songwriter's words.

In perhaps the same way, as colour and shootings around hills and lakes started developing into a critical mass, as Shammi Kapoor and OP Nayyar and all the cast and crew, kings and queens of romance, were making their destinies, we could depend on this quite extraordinary man waving the Jammu & Kashmir flag in such a musically unique and endearing way. His santoor-playing would enhance significantly the mood that the director, cinematographer, in fact all the people who were related to the song or scene wanted to convey.

This is very important, because the mind has associations which are deeply rooted, even if we take many of these for granted. Take away Ustad Bismillah Khan's shehnai from marriage-related songs and see the difference it makes to the ceremonies. Or silence Pandit Ram Narain's sarangi from the many *mujra*s (form of dance originated by courtesans) he has played in, and see the hollowness that leaves behind; it won't help too much either if you replace these with other instruments. *Suno sajna papihe ne* could not have reached the exceptional levels it did, had it also not included Pandit Hariprasad Chaurasia's flute, or *Main piya teri*, without Pandit Pannalal Ghosh's bansuri. It was the same with Pandit Shiv Kumar Sharma's santoor, in a host of film songs.

Facing page: In a lighter vein with director Jabbar Patel during the release of the documentary Antardhvani *on Pandit Shiv Kumar Sharma's life. The film received the Rajat Kamal award.*

A long friendship. In California, with Pandit Ravi Shankar with whom he shared a very personal bond.

But there is a key difference, and this point is being offered without meaning any disrespect to any of the above, as also to Pandit Ravi Shankar and Ustad Vilayat Khan (sitar), Ustad Ali Akbar Khan (sarod), Goody Servai (accordion), among others. The key difference is the fact that all the other instruments have been around the centrestage on India's musical landscape, for generations. Most of the main artistes did exceptional work on their instruments and created wonderful tunes and played wonderful music on them (in and out of cinema). But perhaps none of them had to bear the heavy cross of bringing their instrument out of the backwaters of a part of India, demonstrating that it had the ability to offer sustain (what's called *tthehrao* in Indian music), and glissando (what we call *meend*), and an array of classical features like these. He did this by taking the santoor around in trains and buses.

Now let's look at Shashi Kapoor singing in his shikara in Kashmir, *Pardesiyon se na akhiyaan milaana*, or when Shammi Kapoor goes serenading Sharmila Tagore on the Dal lake, *Taareef karoon kya uski jisne tumhen banaaya*. Neither brother would have quite got the feel of the song without Shivji's santoor lacing the melodies, nor indeed the composers here, Kalyanji-Anandji or OP Nayyar, respectively.

Let's now look into the rear-view mirror and recall some of the many feel-good melodies that were featured in the great outdoors, the ones that had a variety of strokes sensitively executed by Shiv Kumar Sharma. First let's stay in his home state, Jammu & Kashmir, which is where the above two songs were also featured. There was Biswajit weaving a left-hand drive Willy's jeep and wooing Asha Parekh on a cycle, on tree-lined Narbal Road in Srinagar. The song? *Pukaarta chala hoon main* (*Mere Sanam*, 1965). In the same film and in a role reversal, this time it was Asha Parekh chasing Biswajit in the hills: *Jaiye aap kahaan jayenge*, the santoor going along with her too, endorsing her statements. Do recall Rishi Kapoor and Dimple Kapadia in a guest house which happens to be in Pahalgam, with them going *Hum-tum ik kamre mein band hon, aur chaabi kho jaaye*! In the same film, we heard *Main shaayar to naheen*, where after the refrain gets over, Shivji's santoor takes up, and repeats the phrases, the second time washed by a violin ensemble.

The santoor forms the backdrop for Jaiye aap kahaan jayenge, *a song featuring actor Asha Parekh.*

Incidentally, this last santoor in *Bobby* has a heavier tonal quality than the one we normally hear, the reason being that this is not the Indian santoor, this is an Irani one! Shivji was gifted this instrument by the Iranian government, when he visited the country in 1968. He played it in a few other songs too, such as *Mehbooba mehbooba* (*Sholay*, 1975), and his own tune *Lagi aaj saawan ki phir wo jhadi hai* (*Chandni*, 1989). He has preserved that gift till today. Santoor-like instruments, called by different names, exist happily in many parts of the world, as in Iran, Iraq, Hungary, Germany, the USA, China and so on and Shivji has of course played them all. But let's scamper back to his work in cinema. In Kashmir again we have many songs graced with the santoor. We look at *Phir Wohi Dil Laya Hoon* (1963). In a picnic song, Asha Parekh is with her friends in the lap of the mountains, and we see a brook flowing past. Our heroine has a picture of the hero Joy Mukherjee in her hand. And she goes in the raga Kirwani-inspired, *Aankhon se jo utri hai dil mein tasweer hai ik anjaane ki*. In this sensational song, when Asha Bhonsle says, ... *duniya meri,* you hear the santoor filler. ... *badal gayi* proceeds she, and the santoor trills along solo again. In a few seconds your heart is sold to this experience. In the same film, we have Joy and Asha comparing notes about how much they have done for the other. *Zulf ki chhaon mein chehre ka ujaala lekar, teri veeraan si raaton ko jalaaya humne.* After every line that ends with the word *humne* (the rhyme word, as this is a ghazal), the santoor comes through again and again, a pattern repeated through the song, with amazingly euphonic results.

The santoor helped to create some sensational songs for Hindi cinema, made all the more memorable by film actors Asha Parekh (top), Kalpana Kartik and Shammi Kapoor (middle) and Dev Anand (bottom).

We head for Darjeeling and find Shammi Kapoor trying his fortune with Kalpana. The song starts with Rafi's ad-lib *Zara thehro* ... kept company by just the santoor ... *Zara thehro, sada mere dilki zara sunte jaana* ... the santoor solo trill continues ... *Khuli palak mein jhoottha gussa, band palak mein pyaar, jeena bhi mushkil, marna bhi mushkil.* Love and mischief intended and achieved so well, setting the mood for the rest of the song in the hills.

Let's move on to Himachal Pradesh, to the hill station Dalhousie, and meet with Dev Anand being turned on by Nanda: *Aise to na dekho ke humko nasha ho jaye*, goes Rafi on Dev. And we have an ensemble of the santoor, taar shehnai, glockenspiel and violins master planned by Dada Burman, the film being *Teen Deviyan* (1965).

We see ever so many films in the great outdoors (not just in hill stations), and we find the santoor helping to enrich the melodic content of a song. *Kabhi raat-din hum door the, din-raat ka ab saath hai,* go lovers Shashi Kapoor and Sharmila Tagore in *Aamne Saamne* (1967), and the santoor goes with them.

It's songs like these that had maestro Khayyam impressed too. So then when he planned the music for *Aakhri Khat* (1967), he

Top: With Rahul, Pandit Ravi Shankar and Prabha Gopal in California. Above: Actor Hema Malini rendering the phenomenal Ai dil-e-naadaan, *which had the santoor excelling itself.*

engaged a critical Lata Mangeshkar song with Shivji's santoor, and why not? The song was a celebration of nature, in the Kulu valley. *Bahaaro, mera jeevan bhi sanwaaro* starts with Shivji's santoor, then it's laced by a short santoor-sitar dialogue and then these two are joined by a flute, after which the *theka* (supporting composition) starts. It's an experience that has to be visited again and again. Needless to say, Khayyam was ecstatic with the results. No wonder he urged Shivji to help host his party in ever so many songs, including the phenomenal *Ai dil-e-naadaan*, from *Razia Sultan* (1982), with the santoor excelling itself in that unforgettable tune.

Hemant Kumar too was delighted with the rewards the santoor gave him when he made Lata sing *Sapne suhaane ladakpan ke* in *Bees Saal Baad* (1962). The same year Asha Bhonsle had the santoor's soft company in *Meri jaan o meri jaan achha nahin itna sitam*, in Hemant's tune for *Sahib Bibi Aur Ghulam* (1962), only to have Shivji play his instrument for Hemant again in the Lata-rendered *Zindagi kitini khubsurat hai*, in *Bin Badal Barsaat*, next year in 1963. So beside himself was the maestro-filmmaker, he even offered the dashing Shiv the hero's role in his next, Geetanjali Films project. The story was going to centre on a santoor player. 'So what do you say, young man?'

Maybe you guessed Shivji's answer too ... a thumbs-down no thank you Sir! That's how this bridge was crossed, predictably.

Such an offer also came from Shakti Samanta, who had been thrilled by the man and his sounds, heard in his films such as *Kashmir Ki Kali* (1964), in *Ye chaand sa roshan chehra*, and *Sawan Ki Ghata* (1966), in *Aaj koi pyaar se dil ki baaten keh gaya, haaye.* Same response, thank you Sir, but I am on a mission!

This offer could not have come from Dada Burman, of course, since he was a singer and composer only, but it is easy to empathise with the feelings of everyone in whose objectives lay the need to create a great tune. Think of *Jeevan ki baghiya mehkegi*, composed by SD Burman, feelingly delivered by Kishore and Lata ... with its music now, what can one say? Just consider that a man and woman (Mumtaz and Dev Anand in the film), married and in love, are expecting their first baby. The feeling can be heavenly and that feeling had to be translated into music. So we have the first interlude with the santoor and flute trilling along to lead us to the stanza: *Wo mera hoga* (followed by a santoor filler) ... *wo sapna tera hoga* (santoor filler) ... *mil-jul ke maanga wo tera-mera hoga* (santoor filler) ... *jab-jab wo muskuraayega apna savera hoga, wo mera hoga* (santoor) and so it proceeds. We are trying to map a part of the song and get scientific about what is essentially an art. And in this art, that wonderful maestro and his arranger (whoever it was in the film, decided to locate the santoor at these places, so appealingly too). Yes, arrangers, who help decide which instrument is to be included in a song, where a certain instrument will play, what and for how long, solo or ensemble, are critical; these refinements are not so known to many of us, but they have much worth in them.

The strains of the santoor bring alive the performance of actors Mumtaz (top), Shammi Kapoor with Sharmila Tagore (middle) and Dev Anand with Mumtaz (bottom).

Naushad just didn't know how to compromise with music. When he called Shivji to the studios, he had thought it all through. His invitations were not so that the two could compare notes about which theatre they had stayed near in their days of struggle. Perhaps they weren't even aware of the other man's story. But Naushad saab called Shivji to play in the twin songs, *Mere mehboob tujhe meri muhabbat ki qasam*, rendered by Rafi or Lata in *Mere Mehboob* (1963). For these

Actor Rajinder Kumar in Mere Mehboob, *the film with the hit song,* Mere mehboob tu he meri muhabbat ki qasam.

songs, the composer wanted the minimalistic use of instruments and so it was just the santoor and tabla, whatever else you heard in the song was very low-profile indeed.

And so, that's how the inseparable world of Shiv Kumar Sharma and his santoor came to tighten its vice-like grip on us. His work, for much of the sixties and some of the seventies, kept running like a train on two tracks, the tracks here being his work in cinema, and his opus on the concert stage, away from films. Like a master craftsman, he went about weaving his art through both these genres, while overhauling the deep-rooted misconceptions with which so many people had confronted him before, undermining the santoor's abilities. Do recall that a few people had recognised that the man had talent, but it was directed at an instrument that had no chance of displaying any serious classical work, because they believed it wasn't in the nature of the instrument; in fact that it was against its grain.

L to R: Ina Puri, Dilip Kumar, Pandit Shiv Kumar Sharma, Naushad, Pandit Hariprasad Chaurasia, Christine Cipriani and Manjit Bawa at the release of Journey with a Hundred Strings.

Interestingly, after a while of his reputation gaining ground in films, he began to be a little neglectful of concerts and started taking the easy way out. Films were happening and he was busy all the time. The money wasn't bad either. But happily, he soon realised the folly of this neglect. So he corrected his course and swung back into the concert stage again. But then films called him again, in a bigger way, a way that would engage him not just as an instrumentalist, but as a composer, with significantly higher responsibilities.

Your mind does wander around in the world of what-ifs as you consider exceptional songs from the late fifties: what if the santoor was around then? Without meaning to take away from class compositions of the time, what if OP Nayyar had included Shivji's santoor in *Bhool ja ai dil* (Asha Bhonsle/*Hum Sab Chor Hain*, 1956)? After all, you can imagine the santoor's trill sharing the pain we found in Asha's vocals. Songs such as Hemant Kumar's *Ye hasta hua caarvaan* (Hemant and Asha/*Ek Jhalak*, 1957) nag you with similar thoughts.

The santoor is best known in the hills and valleys and where we have water involved, in virtually any way. This can range from lakes and ponds to waterfalls and even spas. But handled well, the notes can sound suspenseful, as they do in *Wo bhooli dastaan;* playful, as in *Achha to hum chalte hain, Pal-bhar ke liye koi humen pyaar karle* and *Dil ka bhanwar kare pukaar;* sad, as in *Dil lagaakar hum ye samjhe* and *Wo jo milte the kabhi;* romantic, as in *Suno sajna* and *Tere husn ki kya taareef karoon;* classical, as in *Pawan deewani, Nainon mein badra chhaye* and *Laaga chunri mein daag.*

Actors Dilip Kumar and Vyjayanthimala enacting the song sequence of Tere husn ki kya taareef karoon.

As a young boy, Shiv had learnt to play the tabla and he had given many performances with it, not just as a child artiste on radio, but as an adult with several music heavyweights, even as he was also playing the santoor. We also saw him find an apartment near the Burmans' home in Bandra, Bombay. One day, RD Burman urged Shivji to play the tabla for his father's upcoming film, *Guide*. Given the scale of that film, it was evident that the song wasn't going to be your garden-variety stuff. And if you want to *hear* that class, do listen to *Mose chhal kiye jaaye, haaye re haaye haaye, dekho, saiyaan beimaan!* It's played by Shiv Kumar Sharma.

Shivji's santoor had been featured in many films of the Chopra banner including *Waqt* and *Humraaz*. Yash Chopra was enjoying the sounds coming out of the instruments played by Hariji (flute) and Shivji (santoor). This bond was being cemented in a variety of ways, including something that happened on the sets of *Humraaz*. The film was a murder-mystery and for a particular scene the filmmaker wanted a specific musical sound of suspense. That wasn't coming through, somehow. At this time, Shivji, casually tinkering with the santoor, playing pizzicato (plucking the strings), produced some notes that caught Yash Chopra's ears. 'What was *that*? Can you play it again?' Yes, this was it, *this* was the sound he was looking for! Such little, little things improved the already good chemistry that existed between them. So much so that the filmmaker would bend over backwards to accommodate them with dates convenient to them. But they just had to be there. (Even now, the signature tune in Yashraj Films features Shivji's santoor, Hariji's flute and Lataji's voice.)

In Mumbai after a concert—Naushad congratulating Rahul.

In the natural course of progression, Shiv and Hari come together to make music for cinema, mostly for the films of Yash Chopra. Just in case you are wondering why together, why not just one of them? The answer is that many people think it's just too much work for one person. And as Shivji was to tell me over a long interview on WorldSpace Satellite Radio, making music for movies is quite difficult, even for two people, much more than concert performances can ever be. You have to forget your role as an instrumentalist and look at the larger picture, and that larger picture is larger by far. Then handling the ever so many people involved, many with giant-size egos. Then there's the lack of discipline and punctuality. Shivji recalls that barring maybe for OP Nayyar, no one used to bother to look at their watches. Amitabh Bachchan though was always punctual—Shiv-Hari got him to sing too. The other thing is about forgetting yourself completely, as in your own preferences. Which is why it seems strange that while both Shivji and Hariji have deep classical roots, clearly out of choice, you don't see any sizeable classical inspirations in their cinema work. That's because you give the producer what he wants. *Jo tum todo piya* is one of the exceptions and its choice was made by Lata Mangeshkar herself. Shivji sang it to her on a harmonium one day after they had recorded *Ye kahaan aa gaye hum*. 'Let's record this bhajan day after tomorrow,' Lata told them.

At the same time, if you want to be successful and respected, then you have to be yourself. This was surely difficult for these two, because they had worked for so many composers, Naushad and C Ramchandra, Hemant Kumar and Ravi, Anil Biswas too, and Shankar-Jaikishen, Khayyam, Madan Mohan, Jaidev, SD Burman and RD Burman, Salil Chowdhury and Ghulam Mohammad, OP Nayyar and Laxmikant-Pyarelal, in lots of songs of Kalyanji-Anandji too. That their work in cinema did not take anything from anyone is also a marvel and this point was made by ace trumpeter Ramprasad Sharma, the father of composer Pyarelal. Consistent with that remark, we see the Meerabai-written Krishna bhajan *Jo tum todo piya*, composed by Shiv-Hari for Lata in *Silsila* (1981), its shades of Chandrakauns a completely different approach from the Bhairavi one in *Jhanak Jhanak Paayal Baje* (1955), with which Shivji was involved at the start of his film career.

L to R: Pandit Hariprasad Chaurasia, Manorama, Rahul, Barkha, actors Amitabh Bachchan and Aishwariya Rai at Rahul's wedding.

Neither did their exposure to off-cinema songs come in the way. Shivji, for instance, had worked in Marathi for Pandit Hridyanath Mangeshkar in *Chaandni Shimpit Jaashi* (Asha Bhonsle), and in Hindi for Manna Dey's composition, so soulfully rendered by Manna Dey, *Ye awaara raaten.*

Shiv-Hari came together not only because the two had worked so much before, on the stage and in recordings, but their instruments also gel so well with each other. There's no fusion here, and so not many people are revolted. But more than all that, there's this fantastic tuning between the two men; they had hit it off with each other very soon and absolutely remain till today a mutual-admiration society. So the Shiv-Hari team for films was formed, and nobody was complaining.

Their first film was *Silsila*, released in 1981, and it was a hit. But even before that, just after two songs were recorded, the composers were flooded with offers, because news travels fast and we must transport

Shiv-Hari's long association with Yash Chopra led to memorable music compositions that struck a chord not merely with the masses but equally with the followers of classical music.

I have known Shivji for over four decades and always admired his music as much as the person. Later I invited Shivji and Hariji to compose music for my films and the rest was musical history. Some great songs, some unforgettable music was created that still enchants listeners.

Yash Chopra

Pandit Hariprasad Chaurasia and Rekha at Barkha and Rahul's wedding.

ourselves to that time to remember that Hindi cinema music was giving a terrible performance in those years. This music, once in riches, was as if in rags. These were times of discordant disco music and dubious musicians. The movie themes too, by and large, were jarring in their content and dialogue. Shiv-Hari's music as such has to be seen from the prism of those times. In a world of rags, their music offered melodies with respectable clothes on.

One of the songs recorded for the film was the Kishore Kumar-Lata Mangeshkar song *Dekha ek khwaab to ye silsile hue*. There is an interesting story to this one. When Yash Chopra called Kishore to ask him to meet Shiv-Hari for a song in the film, the singer turned down the request immediately. '*Naheen ji, inke saath main naheen gaoonga. Ye classical musicians hain, ye mujhe phasa lenge!*' The singer was told not to worry, a cassette would be sent to him soon, a sort of cover version of the song if you like, in Shivji's voice. 'Then you decide.' That song, however beautifully composed, is a Dogri folk song, quite linear in delivery, without the twists that Kishore had feared.

Actors Amitabh Bachchan and Rekha in the film Silsila *for which the santoor helped to popularise the song,* Dekha ek khwaab to ye silsile hue.

In that film Shiv-Hari also got Amitabh Bachchan to sing three songs! *Rang barse bheege chunarwaali rang barse* is a Holi song written by his father Harivansh Rai Bachchan. He also sang the tandem song *Neela aasmaan so gaya*, as also the duet with Lata, *Ye kahaan aa gaye hum*. Amitabh was quite reluctant to sing *Neela aasmaan*, but Yash Chopra put a lot of pressure on the actor, so the latter relented. Shivji recalls, 'Once Amitabh had said yes, he got very serious. He would finish his shoots say around midnight. Then he would sit with us and rehearse till three or four in the morning. And if the recording was at 9 am at the new HMV Studio in World Trade Centre, Cuffe Parade (which it was), the other side of town, you can bet Amitabh would be there by that time.'

The other significant song mentioned above and composed by the duo was the Lata-Amitabh rendered *Ye kahaan aa gaye hum*. The wonderful thing standing out in this one is that Amitabh speaks out his part and Lata sings out hers. Both the artistes as such are made to do what suits them best. The arty use of the female chorus in the interludes and the heartwarming lush use of the violins only make watching the song such a synchronously enjoyed experience.

Shiv-Hari not only had Amitabh sing for them, but also Anupam Kher, in a children's song in *Vijay* (1988): *Akkad bakkad bambe bo*. Later in *Chandni* (1989), he also had Sridevi sing, even if many people feel she should have been left alone to just act, which she did pretty well! The duet she attempted with Jolly Mukherjee was *Rang bhare baadal se.* A couple of other songs in that film had this Punjab throb of rhythms: *Parbat se kaali ghata takraayi* (Asha and Vinod Rathod), and the chorus-backed Lata hit, *Mere haathon mein nau-nau choodiyaan hain, zara thehro sajan majbooriyaan hain.*

In their composing efforts, the duo used plenty of interesting instruments, for example the sarod in *Vijay* (1988): *Tera karam hi teri vijay hai* (Mahendra Kapoor), and in *Jo tum todo piya* in *Silsila*, (1981); santoor, as in *Meri bindiya, teri nindiya* (Lata), and *Kabhi main kahoon* (Lata, Hariharan), both from *Lamhe* (1991). Also in *Faasle* (1985), in *In aankhon ke zeenon se* (Kishore).

They worked with the poetry of Javed Akhtar and Hasan Kamal (*Silsila*), Anand Bakshi (*Chandni, Lamhe* and *Darr*), Nida Fazli in *Vijay*, and Shahryar in *Faasle*. They offered folk tunes with *Dekha ek khwaab to ye silsile hue* (Kishore, Lata/*Silsila*) and *Morni baagaan maan bole* (Lata, Ila Arun) as well as *Megha re megha re tera man tarsa re* (Lata, Ila Arun), both from *Lamhe*. While the festival of Holi was turned musical earlier as we saw Amitabh sing *Rang barse bheege chunarwaali* and later *Ang se ang lagaana* (*Darr*), rendered by Alka Yagnik, Devika Pandit, Vinod Rathod and Sudesh Bhonsle, all backed by chorus.

Aadhi raat ko palkon ki chhaon mein, went Lata and Amit Kumar, in *Parampara* (1993). Saif played the piano and to match him, Aamir got on to the drums. Exceptional work by Shiv-Hari's team in the recording room, but a pinch-of-salt situation cinematically. Naturally, the actors' shots were taken from a distance.

Kaise jeeyoonga main, agar tu na bani meri saahibaan, went Jolly Mukherjee and Anuradha Paudwal in Ramesh Talwar's *Sahiban*, released in 1993, nicely tuned by Shiv and Hari near the end of their composing work in films.

Darr (1993) had many exceptional tracks such as *Jaadu teri nazar*, with Udit in super company with the guitar too. But this one rendered by Udit Narayan and Lata was something else: *Tu mere saamne, main tere saamne, tujhko dekhoon ke pyaar karoon ... toot gayi toot gayi main choor ho gayi.* In this song, look at the beautiful planning, so pleasing to the ears: Udit sings in the minor scale, while Lata's rendition is in major. But they merge seamlessly; it's a clear case of intelligent imagination at work.

As time went by Shiv Kumar Sharma and Hariprasad Chaurasia started getting even more busy with their concerts. Then came a tipping-point situation. After just such a run of performances in April and May, Shivji returned from the US in June and headed to Srinagar with his family for a month's vacation. The next day he got a call from Yash Chopra, 'Shivji, please write down the words of this song, *Lagi aaj saawan ki phir wo jhadi hai*. Anand Bakshi has written the song and I have got Vinod Khanna's dates. Please come back tomorrow.'

In Mumbai, at a programme as Chief Guest with actors Rani Mukherji and Hema Malini.

Shivji told the filmmaker, 'Yashji, I can't come tomorrow. But give me three to four days, let me see, I will compose something. There's a lot of rush for tickets just now.'

The filmmaker didn't have time to think about that 'rush' for tickets. He believed in 'Yash' for tickets! That very evening a local travel agent landed up where Shivji was staying. He handed over tickets for them to fly out the next day! As for Hariji now, he was in Holland and he too had to cut short his stay. The song was composed and then rendered by Suresh Wadkar and Anupama. It clicked, but the composers had to pay a price for it, that being their vacation. The constant pressure on their time was getting difficult to handle. The musicians were getting more busy, performing quite routinely away from each other at various points of the globe. For the complex film work, however, they *both* had to be around, in Mumbai and at the same time.

Which brings us up to the music story of *Dil To Paagal Hai*. The film's music was planned with Shiv and Hari first. But this film got somewhat delayed in the making, about four months or so. The screenplay too had got changed for some reason. Yash Chopra asked the composing duo to accommodate him this time. 'I have been working around your dates for so long. You adjust this time for me, cancel your concerts abroad.' His request didn't seem unfair, but how could they adjust? Shivji told the filmmaker that was impossible as there was a contractual obligation with the Americans. Some thirty concerts had been planned out over months. They would sue him and it would be curtains for him and his reputation. Then Yash Chopra asked if they could compose just one or two songs for this film. But even that was hard, since the maestros were walking on the tightrope of time. That's how they had to decline making the music for *Dil To Paagal Hai*.

We need to come to one more bridge, of them deciding what they wanted to do next, what with so much pressure on their time both within cinema and outside it. As it is, they had stayed in it for so long, a real marvel of an achievement by any yardstick. Other classical musicians such as Ali Akbar Khan and Pandit Ravi Shankar had made music in films, but not in so many of them. In a way it's like riding a boat with two hulls, a sort of music catamaran. Only in a real catamaran, both the hulls face the same direction and have a common forward objective. Here, just the fact that it was music was common. The hulls were quite divergent in their objectives. It is therefore that this composing duo decided to call it a day in films.

We can see clearly that they had done their work, in the 'low' decade of the 1980s, going against the conventional 'music' that was being churned out then. In their wake, they had helped pave the way for healthy music coming out of our cinema again, in films such as *Ashiqui, Maine Pyar Kiya, Hum Aapke Hain Koun* and more.

After leaving, they went back to concerts and classical. The two kept giving performances and do so still—cutting discs and winning hearts. They both have able sons who have taken up after their fathers. Shivji himself is seventy-five, with his feet firmly on the ground, while his creativity and imagination is right up there, zero-gravity, just like his riveting hairdo. Here is a man who remembers by first name almost any person that he met for a few minutes even once. He engages with

Before a concert in Mumbai with actor Juhi Chawla playing the tanpura.

such people interactively, even as he somehow finds the time and space to rise into the clouds and plan his next composition to wow the audience once again.

Yes, he left or declined many things and opportunities in his remarkable life. But one thing he has not left and which has not left him either, is his santoor. To people like me, bred excessively on film music, Shivji's leaving films is a big loss, both his playing the santoor and composing melodies. But I remain an optimist; who knows, if a good film comes along, perhaps he will not say, 'No thank you'!

Some of the songs for which Shiv Kumar Sharma played the santoor:

Song	**Singer**	**Film and year**
Aapne kya kaha, maine kya sun liya	Lata	*Aaya Toofan* (1964)
Aaya re khilonewaala	Rafi	*Bachpan* (1970)
Achha to hum chalte hain	Lata, Kishore	*Aan Milo Sajna* (1970)
Baad muddat ke ye ghadi aayi	Rafi, Suman	*Jahan Ara* (1964)
Baagon mein kaise ye phool	Lata, Mukesh	*Chupke Chupke* (1975)
Bindiya chamkegi	Lata	*Do Raaste* (1969)
Chaand si mehbooba ho meri	Mukesh	*Himalay Ki God Mein* (1965)
Chalo sajna jahaan tak ghata chale	Lata	*Mere Humdum Mere Dost* (1968)
Chhoo lene do naazuk hontthon ko	Rafi	*Kaajal* (1965)
Dekha ek khwaab to ye silsile hue	Kishore, Lata	*Silsila* (1981)
Dil ka bhanwar kare pukaar	Rafi	*Tere Ghar Ke Saamne* (1963)
Dil lagaakar hum ye samjhe	Mahendra Kapoor	*Zindagi Aur Maut* (1965)
Ek ajnabi haseena se	Kishore	*Ajnabi* (1974)

Song	Singer	Film and year
Ek chameli ke mandve tale	Asha, Rafi	*Cha Cha Cha* (1964)
Ek tu jo mila, saari duniya mili	Lata	*Himalay Ki God Mein* (1965)
Haaye re haaye, neend naheen aaye	Lata, Rafi	*Humjoli* (1970)
Hai tere saath meri wafa	Lata	*Hindustan Ki Qasam* (1973)
Hum jab simatke aapki baahon mein	Asha, Mahendra Kapoor	*Waqt* (1965)
Humne to dilko aapke qadmon pe	Rafi, Asha	*Mere Sanam* (1965)
Humne tujhko pyaar kiya hai jitna	Lata	*Dulha Dulhan* (1964)
In aankhon ke zeenon se	Kishore, Lata	*Faasle* (1985)
Itna hai tumse pyaar mujhe mere	Rafi, Suman	*Suraj* (1966)
Jaane kya sochkar naheen guzra	Kishore	*Kinaara* (1977)
Jeevan se bhari teri aankhen	Kishore	*Safar* (1970)
Kabhi main kahoon	Lata, Hariharan	*Lamhe* (1991)
Kaheen ek maasoom naazuk si ladki	Rafi	*Shankar Husain* (1977)

Song	Singer	Film and year
Karoge yaad to har baat yaad aayegi	Bhupinder	*Bazaar* (1982)
Khilte hain gul yahaan	Lata/Kishore	*Sharmilee* (1971)
Kise raah mein kisi mod par	Lata, Mukesh	*Mere Humsafar* (1974)
Laaga chunri mein daag	Manna Dey	*Dil Hi To Hai* (1963)
Laakhon hain nigaah mein	Rafi	*Phir Wohi Dil Laaya Hoon* (1963)
Main teri nazar ka suroor hoon	Talat	*Jahan Ara* (1964)
Main to har mod par tujhko doonga sada	Mukesh	*Chetna* (1970)
Mehndi lagi mere haath re	Lata	*Mehndi Lagi Mere Haath* (1962)
Meri bindiya teri nindiya	Lata	*Lamhe* (1991)
Meri muhabbat jawaan rahegi	Rafi	*Janwar* (1965)
Muhabbat ke suhaane din	Rafi	*Maryada* (1971)
Nainon mein badra chhaaye	Lata	*Mera Saaya* (1966)
Neela aasmaan so gaya	Amitabh Bachchan	*Silsila* (1981)
O mere dil ke chain	Kishore	*Mere Jeevan Saathi* (1972)

Song	Singer	Film and year
O sanam tere ho gaye hum	Lata, Rafi	*Ayee Milan Ki Bela* (1964)
Pal-bhar ke liye koi humen	Kishore, Usha Khanna	*Johnny Mera Naam* (1970)
Patta-patta boota-boota	Lata, Rafi	*Ek Nazar* (1972)
Pawan deewaani	Lata	*Dr Vidya* (1962)
Phoolon ke rang se	Kishore	*Prem Pujari* (1970)
Suno sajna	Lata	*Aan Milo Sajna* (1966)
Tere bina soone nain hamaare	Rafi, Lata	*Meri Surat Teri Aankhen* (1963)
Tere husn ki kya taareef karoon	Rafi, Lata	*Leader* (1964)
Tere mere sapne ab ek rang hain	Rafi	*Guide* (1965)
Tum agar saath deneka waada karo	Mahendra Kapoor	*Humraaz* (1967)
Wo bhooli daastaan	Lata	*Sanjog* (1961)
Wo jo milte the kabhi	Lata	*Akeli Mat Jaiyo* (1963)
Zindagi ke safar mein guzar jaate hain	Kishore	*Aap Ki Kasam* (1974)

EPILOGUE

My Dad, My Guru

Each time I've been asked to write a few words about my father, I wonder how is it possible to interpret or express a relationship between a guru/father and disciple/son. Well, to me he's my father first and then a guru.

Having heard several times from my dad about how he arrived in Mumbai from Jammu in the sixties to embark upon a musical career and introduce the santoor to the world, one can gather that he obviously was not afraid of taking risks and had his goals well set. To say that his journey has been inspiring is an understatement, it's the kind of stuff that sells autobiographies. The santoor is what it is today thanks to one man's efforts and I am proud to inherit it from him. He started teaching me when I was twelve and I began seeing him in dual roles—a father and a guru. I could learn several virtues from him apart from music, such as patience, focus, discipline and, above all, a spiritual contentment, which comes only when there is inner peace.

13 January 2013, Pandit Shiv Kumar Sharma's seventy-fifth birthday. L to R: Rohit, Manorama, granddaughter Ananya, Rahul, Barkha and Mayuri.

My dad has always been happily surprised with my world music collaborations and has always encouraged me to try out something different, yet maintain the tradition. It is also a quality in progressive people to move on in life and leave the past behind.

He has such a positive outlook in life and from him I have learnt that it is actually the only way to be happy. I have seldom found him dejected or negative.

Every person has an aura and there are few who radiate peace and calm as well as spirituality and yet are winners in their fields. My dad is one of them.

Rahul Sharma

Index

Contributors

Vijay Kichlu started initial training in music at the age of five from Pandit Nathuram Sharma. Later, he was greatly influenced by the style of singing of Ustad Faiyyaz Khan, the colossus of the Agra *gharana*. He had the good fortune of becoming a disciple of the famous Dagar Brothers—Ustad Moinuddin Dagar and Ustad Aminuddin Dagar.

A fluent speaker, Vijay has made significant contribution to important musicological meets all over the world and is the recipient of the Sangeet Natak Academy Award, the Kala Vipanchi, the Sangeet Ratna and the Sangeet Bharati, among other special awards. He set up and managed Sangeet Research Academy as its Executive Director for twenty-four years.

Manek Premchand is fascinated by the enormous role that cinema has played as a key medium in a country as diverse as India. This fascination has motivated him to write three books on the subject—*Yesterday's Melodies, Today's Memories; Musical Moments from Hindi Films* and *Romancing the Song*. This last is a seminal work that takes a deep look at lyrics down the years; the University of California has made this book a primary reference and teaching source in its subject 'Bollywood and Beyond'. In April 2013, he was felicitated by Manipal University, Karnataka, for this path-breaking research on lyrics in Hindi cinema.

He presented a one-day event, '100 Years of Indian Cinema—A Musical Journey', in association with Bharatiya Vidya Bhavan, Mumbai.